THE RETURN OF INSPECTOR PIRAT

His first book

Edition 1.2 – March 07 2016

ISBN - 9781511429467

© Rob Falconer 2015

Rob Falconer has asserted his right under the Copyright, Designs and Patents Act 1988 to be the identified as the author of this work

All rights reserved

Visit the author's website:
www.robertfalconer.co.uk/

Index

Chapter 1 – Snow Job

Chapter 2 – One-way Ticket

Chapter 3 – Cinéma Vérité

Chapter 4 – On the Warpath

Chapter 5 – The Milk of Human Unkindness

Chapter 6 – The Little Lady Vanishes

Chapter 7 – Downwardly Mobile

Chapter 8 – Get Off the Earth

Chapter 9 – A Load of Old Rubbish

Chapter 10 – Going for Baroque

Chapter 11 – Abracadaver

Chapter 12 – A Hostile Reception

Chapter 13 – Grotesquerie

Chapter 14 – A Surfeit of Shoes

Chapter 15 – Foul Whisperings

Chapter 16 – Justice is Done

Chapter 17 – Upstairs and Downstairs, and in My Lady's Chamber

Chapter 18 – Casualty of War

Chapter 19 – Truck Stop

Chapter 20 – Another Brick in the Wall

Epilogue

Snow Job

When John Holmes got to the top of the main chair-lift from Klochers Village to the summit of Mount Mlosc, he found a large group of people gathered around the top of another chair-lift to his right.

Knowing it would be wiser to ignore the situation completely and to continue to the main skiing pistes to his left, he nevertheless sauntered off towards the crowd, perhaps through idle curiosity, perhaps because of the professional interest of a police officer on holiday. "Plain ruddy nosy" would have been the phrase, suitably bowdlerised, his staff would have used.

The chair-lift was stopped, and a rather plump lady in a striking pink-and-white ski outfit was lying on the ground underneath one of the chairs. Someone with at least some medical experience (perhaps another meddlesome professional on holiday, John thought to himself) was crouched over the body, examining it in a rather brisk, perfunctory manner. It seemed dead.

Suddenly a swathe was cut through the crowd as a police officer and his entourage arrived. He quickly questioned the medical person, then the chair-lift attendant, and then, surprisingly, turned to John.

"You must be a policeman from England on holiday, I think?" he asked rhetorically. John hadn't realised that it was so obvious, but then conceded that he could probably have pulled the same trick had he met this foreign police officer in Britain. He nodded. "Can I be of any assistance?" he asked unenthusiastically.

"I am sure you will be valuable," replied Inspector Vasilev (as his name turned out to be). "Mrs. Wolf here is English. Most of the tourists here are English. My English is perhaps not so good in conversation. You could perhaps help me out if anyone from England needs to be grilled."

John had usually found that most of the inhabitants of holiday resorts that catered mainly for British tourists invariably spoke reasonable English, at least within the spheres of their respective trades. However, that rarely seemed to apply to the local police force. He assumed that the reason was that the officers had to act and speak as representatives of their country's law at all times, and could therefore never even contemplate making the slightest error. Surprisingly therefore, Inspector Vasilev seemed happy to converse in English, even if he had obviously learnt most of the technical terms from old American detective films.

John waited whilst the Inspector finished his enquiries with the chair-lift attendant and the medical gentleman (who turned out to be a chiropodist).

The Inspector took him aside. "It looks shut-and-open," he confided. "Mrs. Wolf has been stabbed to the death. The knife, from one of our hotels in the Village I am afraid, was in her chest up to the hilt. But she was alone on the chair-lift when she arrived up here. Petko here," he indicated the young chair-lift attendant, "Says he had just started up the lift, and there had been only one other passenger, a young girl who had been about five chairs in front of Mrs. Wolf. Petko stopped the lift to get poor Mrs. Wolf off, but he checked with the lower station that there weren't any others still on the lift, otherwise he would have restarted it and let them off."

"The knife was well hidden under Mrs. Wolf's ski jacket, so nobody could have thrown the knife at her. We had better go on down to the lower station and have a chat there. I suppose someone could have sat alongside Mrs. Wolf, killed her, and then jumped off the chair-lift near the top. It would have been quite a jump, but just possible at one or two points where the chairs run fairly close to the ground. Based on my experience, I would have said that it *could* have been suicide, but that the position of the knife made it unlikely. Are you coming?" Inspector Vasilev asked as he paced off towards the chair-lift. John realised his answering in the negative had not even been considered.

The fatal chair-lift was one that served a fairly short isolated red run of medium difficulty that started out from the top of the main chair-lift, but which lay in the opposite direction to that of the majority of the ski runs. As Klochers was an East European ski resort 'manufactured' (and renamed) largely for first-time inexperienced British skiers, the slightly more difficult runs were not usually very popular until at least the middle of the week, certainly not early on Monday morning. This particular red run was rarely used much until at least the morning ski tuition classes had finished, or the more foolhardy skiers had awoken from their après-ski-induced sleep.

Just after the lift had started, Inspector Vasilev pointed out an area of disturbed snow below them. "If we are looking for a murderer, I am sure that that is where he would have jumped off. But it's on a curve in the piste below, so the snow could have been churned up" (Inspector Vasilev was clearly pleased with this phrase) "by yesterday's skiers."

For the rest of the short journey down, the Inspector extolled the virtues of his homeland and its scenery. As he became more emotional, his command of English became less proficient. Occasionally, he flung out both arms in a gesture of overwhelming pride: John felt forced to cling tightly to the security bar for safety.

At the bottom of the lift, another, almost-identical, attendant was lounging against a barrier, clearly bored. His name was Petko too, it seemed. Although he was probably only accustomed to using English in the few sentences relevant to his particular job, he was happy enough to conduct the conversation in English for John's sake.

John was surprised to see that Inspector Vasilev already had a Polaroid photograph of Mrs. Wolf. He had seen one of his team using a rather large and cumbersome piece of equipment, but had assumed it to be some forensic laboratory apparatus rather than the very old instant camera that he now realised it was.

Vasilev explained briefly what had happened, and of their suspicions. He showed Petko the photograph.

Petko nodded, "Yes, yes, I am recognising this lady. Before Petko told me to switch off the juice, I had only two chairs in operation. She got on the chair alone."

Both Inspector Vasilev and John asked simultaneously, "You're sure she got on alone?"

Petko was most definite, "Yes, yes, she was on her own in the chair." He frowned a little, and added, "But if she had been murdered, she would have been seen, surely?"

Back in the chair-lift on their way back to the top, the Inspector turned to John, "Look, if he insists that she got into the chair on her own, it must have been suicide. I will continue my investigations, of course, but I can't imagine any reason why the two attendants here might have lied. I can't think there would have been any collusion, either: the staff here don't tend to mix much with the tourists."

"Anyway, I'm sure you want to get on with enjoying your holiday," the Inspector continued with rather more consideration than John had thought him capable of. "If you would care to do me a favour, perhaps you would keep your ear to the floor with the English tourists. If you hear of anyone who's been in Klochers before, or who has some sort of relationship with anyone here, then please inform me r.s.v.p. In return, it will be my pleasure to let you know how things are progressing from up my end."

And indeed John did manage to have a good holiday. It was his first time skiing, and the resort perfectly suited his total lack of ability combined with his rather high level of dignity. In fact, he began to enjoy himself so much that he avoided the après-ski after around nine o'clock in order to get an early night and be up on the slopes as early as possible in the morning.

Inspector Vasilev kept to his word, and sent an officer round each evening to "keep him posted." The Inspector had since questioned the two chair-lift attendants again, but they still maintained that Mrs. Wolf had got on alone and had arrived at the top of Mount Mlosc both alone and dead. He felt certain that there was no reason to consider that they might be involved in any way.

Mr. Wolf he had also "grilled." Not a very nice man, he thought. Mr. Wolf was a relatively successful car dealer from North London with an agency for some imported Oriental cars made not far from Japan: however, he hankered after a BMW agency. When asked if he thought his wife might have any reason to take her life, he suggested that their rapidly-disintegrating marriage might have been at the back of her mind. No, he didn't do it, he said. He didn't have an alibi, but, there again, from what he had heard, he said he thought he wouldn't be needing one.

John did try and ask around to see who knew Mr. and Mrs. Wolf, but few had seen much of them as they had kept apart from the rest of their group. He only learnt that they hadn't seemed to like each other very much at the beginning of the holiday, and that there had been some arguments. However, they had seemed to be getting closer as the week wore on. Mr. Wolf was apparently seen by some as being very charming and persuasive, whilst others thought him unpleasant and not to be trusted, in short, the archetypal car salesman. However, John was aware that his policemanly manner was at such variance with the holiday atmosphere as to deter most people from really opening out to him.

And so John tried to forget Mrs. Wolf, and concentrated on perfecting his skiing technique: at this stage, this consisted of staying upright as much as possible for as long as possible, even if this did usually involve his clutching at other people (some of them quite nice, he thought).

And one of the quite nice people to whom he had clung (not altogether randomly) was Jackie from Sunderland, with whom he was getting quite friendly.

But it was on Wednesday that some things began to fall into place: not with his skiing of course, for that was beyond redemption.

Wednesday morning, Jackie had a slight hangover, and so stayed at the hotel for an extra hour or so. She said she was not going to be good company for at least a while, and so suggested that John go on ahead of her.

At the top of the main chair-lift, he turned to his left, away from the red run that had messed up his holiday to some degree (and, for that matter, Mrs. Wolf's as well, he thought). To his surprise, he saw Jackie ahead of him about to descend an easy run back to the village.

"So where's your headache now, Jackie?" he yelled loudly, for once coming to quite a professional stop alongside her. His superb manoeuvre was wasted: as the girl turned around, he saw that it wasn't Jackie at all. Admittedly, she had similar hair, but that was all: in all other respects she was totally unlike Jackie.

Being a cheap resort with few difficult runs, Klochers attracted first-time skiers who were not as yet committed: hence, they spent less on their ski outfits than those who regularly visited the more professional (and expensive) resorts. Most were kitted out by a well-known chain of clothing stores, and pink was the 'in' colour this year.

Both Jackie and this girl were wearing identical outfits. And he had mistaken this girl for Jackie. After all, only part of the face and some hair were visible.

He wondered if one of the chair-lift attendants had made the same mistake as he had.

He remembered a comment from the lower Petko. He wondered why he was so sure that Mrs. Wolf couldn't have been murdered without having been seen. Had he seen others on the slopes below? There couldn't have been anyone else on the chair-lifts who could have seen anything, surely? The upper Petko had said that there had been a girl alone in the first occupied chair, and his namesake from the bottom chair-lift station had said Mrs. Wolf had got on alone also. As Mrs. Wolf had been to the rear, surely the lower Petko wouldn't have expected her to have been observed by the girl in front.

John was still getting nowhere with his unofficial investigation, so he tried to clear his mind and get on with his skiing.

But Petko's words were obviously still whirling around in his head, for he concentrated less and less on his skiing, and, surprisingly, began to ski better. He found himself positioning his body more as his instructor had suggested, and less as his terror dictated he should. He stopped leaning backwards, as only the children seemed to be able to get away with that. When traversing, he began to lean towards the bottom of the slope instead of away, as some internal sense of preservation usually told him to. And, most surprisingly, he even forgot to feel embarrassed when he fell over.

His preoccupation with Mrs. Wolf's airborne demise thus helped his skiing proficiency immeasurably. It would be unfortunate if he should solve the problem, as his ability to remain vertical on the slopes would probably diminish rapidly.

But it was on Thursday, in mid-traverse, that everything finally fell into place and he realised what must really have happened.

Well, most of it anyway.

The next day he had a chat with Petko at the lower chair-lift station, and then sought out Inspector Vasilev.

He said he was all ears.

"There was only ever one real suspect, but I now *know* that Mr. Wolf murdered his wife."

"But how?" interrupted Inspector Vasilev. "The chair-lift attendants are adamant she got on alone, and that she was alone when she reached the top. Are you suggesting some collusion between the husband and the attendant at the lower station?"

John shook his head.

"No. Mr. Wolf must have gone skiing down that red run early on the first day. He probably had little to persuade him to stay with his wife in the hotel. He spotted a girl with the same build as his wife, wearing exactly the same outfit: he may even have thought it was his wife at first. He got chatting to her, and found that she intended to start skiing there at the same time the next day as well. He may even have arranged a rendezvous with her."

"On the fatal morning, he managed to convince his wife that she should accompany him skiing: their relationship seemed to be improving, and he could be very persuasive. He waited for this other girl to ski ahead of them down the red run: if he had arranged a rendezvous with her and she had seen him, he would have merely pointed at his wife, mouthed some silent apology, and ignored the girl from then on. The tricky bit, as far as he was concerned, was how to induce his wife to get onto the chair-lift without her ski jacket: surprisingly, it rarely seems cold here, but he would have had to be have been pretty persuasive to get her to remove it. Perhaps he had some sort of bet whether she could stand the cold, or perhaps he was holding it whilst she adjusted the rest of her clothing. He would have thought of something, I'm sure."

"The girl would have got onto the chair-lift first, alone of course. The chair-lift attendant would later testify that Mrs. Wolf, actually someone wearing the same ski outfit as she had, had got on alone."

"Mr. and Mrs. Wolf then boarded the chair-lift about five chairs after this lone girl. The attendant wouldn't have bothered to mention the woman without a jacket who got on later with a man who was carrying her ski jacket inside out."

"Once Mrs. Wolf had put her jacket on again, her husband stabbed her, and then jumped off near the summit (a reasonably easy feat, as we've agreed)."

Inspector Vasilev shifted thoughtfully in his seat, "O.K. If we have a word with our friend Petko and go over things in more detail, I'm sure we'll be able to match what you say happened with his statement. We shouldn't have too much trouble hunting for this girl in pink, either."

He clapped his hands. "Yes," he said rather loudly. He seemed pleased.

John was less pleased. While he had spent all this time helping the Police with their enquiries, Jackie had switched her attentions to a chartered accountant from Hemel Hempstead.

Interval

Nigella Ingledew sought out her tutor, Tony Harrison, in a corner of the Students' Union bar.

"Do you know Professor Guiteras well?" she asked.

Her tutor smiled. "I thought you'd be one of the ones he'd pick."

Nigella's face obviously registered her disappointment: "You know about it?"

He nodded and smiled, and then continued, "Every year, our Professor Guiteras winkles out those who show some interest in detective stories. He then invites them to what I've heard is a truly sumptuous buffet at this house for an evening in celebration of detective fiction. He's had a few of his stories published in his native, er, Spain, I suppose. Everyone attending has to read out an original story they've written specially. Have you prepared yours yet?"

"Well, I've written it, but I'm not too sure about it. Couldn't I just 'borrow' one from a book?" Nigella ventured.

"You'd better not. Some student tried it once. She borrowed a short story by

Edmund Crispin based on the fact that 'rowed' and 'rode' have the same sounds. She didn't seem to realise that our Professor Guiteras has read just about every detective story ever written: she would have had to have found something really obscure to have fooled him."

"Anyway, he knew the story. He thoroughly humiliated her in front of all her fellow-students, and she left his house in tears."

"Well, I've written a story about someone murdered at a ski resort. Can I read it to you?" Nigella asked. "You could let me know whether you think it's good enough, Tony."

Tony leaned back and closed his eyes.

"Read on," he said.

Professor Guiteras lived in an old three-storey semi-detached house in a street consisting solely of similar buildings. All the others had long since been converted into flats for student accommodation, and his was the only one still intact.

Nigella could have located the house merely by examining the décor visible through the upstairs windows. Professor Guiteras' was the only house to have paintings rather than large colour posters adorning the walls. The front door was wide open, and, by the sound of gentle conversation coming from the interior, she realised she was not the first to arrive.

Indeed, she was the last.

"Ah, my dear," Professor Guiteras bestowed three syllables upon this last word, "Do have a drink. You're the last, but not to worry. My wife is still preparing the table, and so perhaps we should start the entertainment. I think I've invited rather too many to my soiree, but it is such a good year, such a good year, and I didn't want to leave any of you out."

"I think you all know the reason for your being here. I adore detective fiction, and I think that all of you share my love. I feel sure that all of you are capable of constructing a fine story in the tradition of the Masters. As payment, I am afraid all I can offer is some fine food and some even finer wines."

"So, who would like to make a start? Nigella, perhaps ...?"

During the Professor's opening speech, most of the students there had gradually started moving towards the far end of the room, as if subconsciously trying to recreate the same atmosphere as at his lectures, or perhaps just trying not to be chosen first.

As the last to arrive, Nigella had remained near the door, and decided it might be thought rude to move into the rear of the room until the Professor had finished his introduction. She was therefore nearest to Professor Guiteras when he selected her to read the first story. As with many people, she was never quite sure whether it was the best policy to be first, last, or near the middle, so the Professor's deciding for her suited her.

She began her story.

She felt conscious that she was talking a little too fast, and perhaps not stressing the salient points as well as she should. When she had finished, she could sense that her fellow-students felt unsure what to do, as they were never expected to show any reaction after Professor Guiteras' lectures. After an uncomfortable few seconds, the students politely and rather quietly applauded. Nigella thought that the later stories might receive louder applause, perhaps because the audience would feel more relaxed as the evening wore on, but more likely because of the wine consumed.

Her tale over, Nigella slowly moved towards the back of the room, determined to remain as inconspicuous as possible for the remainder of the evening, and just to enjoy the food and wine.

"Excellent," Professor Guiteras said, rising to his feet: he had chosen a comfortable chair, which the students had supposed to be a favourite, and had avoided. "I think my wife is still not quite ready, so perhaps we can squeeze in another story before eating."

"Simon …?" he entreated.

The Professor called upon Simon Woolway to 'deliver his sermon' as he put it (rather too tweely, Nigella thought).

Nigella wondered if 'tweely' were a real word.

Simon began …

One-way Ticket

It was damp and quite dark in the small valley below the village. It was early one wet August morning, and the drizzle hung over the moist earth like a net curtain, dimming the already-weak street lighting that occasionally filtered through the trees from the road above. There was very little to be heard in the little valley, the only natural sound being a soft gurgle that could be traced to a little stream nearby.

Seemingly centre-stage, in the middle of a lurid splash of gently-buzzing light, stood a large high-floor touring coach, its engine stopped and its interior lighting shining futilely onto the surrounding wasteland. The passenger door was open and light spilled down the steps.

A middle-aged man wearing a navy blue blazer lay unmoving inside the coach, his body half-sprawled down the steps. There was a gash on the side of his head. It was quite deep, and some of his blood spilled down the steps, mingling with the now-dimming but still insistently-buzzing fluorescent light …

Llandrofa was a small village at the top end of one of the South Wales mining valleys. Even at the height of the coal boom, it had never been very important, and it now offered hardly any employment at all, most of those under thirty-five having joined a mass exodus to the more prosperous coastal townships where almost everyone only spoke English.

Situated in the narrowest part of the valley, the village had only space for one main road (grandly called The Avenue), and even that petered out at the far end into a waste area solely visited by sheep and old mattress discarders. Apart from little spurs of terraced houses running laterally off this thoroughfare, the only other road in the village was a small lane serving a thin strip of allotments: this ran parallel to The Avenue, but slightly lower, in a small dip before the steep walls of the valleys began. It was separated from the other streets by an area of thick foliage and bushes, through which the local children, at least those still too young to seek employment elsewhere, had forced a number of alleyways and paths.

The coach was such an incongruous sight in the narrow lane that it would naturally attract the attention of the first person to use the lane. Normally, it seems that such discoveries are made by some early dog-walking citizen, but most canine pets roam free all night in Llandrofa, and the dead man was not discovered until around ten a.m. by Mr. E. B. Jones, who was on his way to check that his vegetables hadn't been vandalised. The following Saturday was the day of the local fete, and one of E. B. Jones' carrots had won the "Most Grotesque Vegetable of the Year" award for the last three years.

"I didn't realise Chip Jenkins had any coaches he could send abroad," said Detective Gerald Williams, "... well, not humanely, anyway. My kids go to school on one of his old bangers, and they reckon that's why he's called Chip ... it's short for Chipolata."

Detective Brian Probert added "My Kevin reckons they're death-traps ..." His voice trailed off quietly.

Their superior officer had already been on the telephone to Eli 'Chip' Jenkins, the coach's operator. "Apparently, Eli's just bought an executive coach from some firm near London. I think it's quite a few years old, but very well-appointed, or so he told me. He's hoping to break into the continental tours market, and this was his first trip. I'm not sure if he'll feel up to running any more now, under the circumstances."

"Anyway, Llandrofa Christian Unity Choir, against the better judgement of some of the committee members I would add, hired the coach from him to go to some festival near Amsterdam. I know most of the members of the choir through Rotary and the Church, and they're pretty respectable. The driver seemed all right too. He was a local man, married, no convictions or children, around forty-two or so. I gather there was quite a bit of rivalry amongst the regular drivers to do this job, but Eli selected him because he said he had some experience of continental coaching, although I'm not too sure that was true: he'd probably only been on a day trip to Calais."

"You'd better have a chat with Eli and the Choir secretary, and see what you can dig up."

Eli Jenkins' yard looked as if he never sold or disposed of anything. The carcasses of old buses, cars, lorries, agricultural machinery, and other unidentifiable pieces of mechanical equipment lay quietly rotting at the far end of the old farmyard, occasionally being added to, and gradually overwhelming the yard. The new coach was still away, being examined by Forensics, and the remainder of the fleet presented a rather depressing aspect.

Eli Jenkins was to be found in an antiquated railway wagon minimally adapted as an office. Over the entrance was a large sign, "Albatross Continental Luxury Coach Tours." The name had been the result of a competition Eli Jenkins had run for the drivers to suggest a name for the new venture (he had only just rejected the suggested "Titanic Transcontinental"). The sign had obviously been painted in situ, as the letters had run slightly, giving the sign a slightly ghoulish look.

The 'office' had a computer and a fax machine, but old oil drums doubled as chairs. Eli Jenkins was balanced surprisingly comfortably on the most commodious-looking oil drum. "David Jenkins, no relation of course, said he'd had experience of continental driving, so I thought I'd use him to spearhead my push into Europe. I wanted to develop it to complement my schools contracts, so the church choir outing was a real godsend. I'll be producing a Tours leaflet next month. Do you want me to send you both some copies?"

Inspectors Williams and Probert said yes, no, er, maybe.

"I'm mainly interested in hearing about David Jenkins, actually" said Gerald Williams.

"David? He hasn't … hadn't been working here long. He's married, seemed fairly reliable."

"Any money worries?" asked Williams.

"He's got a mortgage. No more than most of my drivers, I suppose."

"Had he ever been to Belgium, or Amsterdam in particular, *before*?" asked Williams, in a manner he obviously thought seemed incisive.

"I have to say honestly that I don't really know. There was a lot of competition amongst the drivers to take this first trip into Europe, and, of course, they all wanted to be Captain of the new coach. I bought David a new blazer you know, navy blue it was, with all the epaulettes and gold braid - well, I went halves with him anyway - so the whole outfit really looked tasteful and professional. I was going to buy a naval hat with 'Captain' written on it, but David wasn't too sure about that. I reckon it would have set it all off nicely, though," Eli Jenkins mused.

"Anyway, some of the other drivers said they'd done some continental driving, but it was only David whose claims had any real credibility. He knew they drove on the other side of the road in Holland, and, when I mentioned Amsterdam, he said that he'd spent a few weekends there when he was younger, and that he really knew the area well. In fact, he told me quite poetically about all the beautiful old buildings there, and the canals with their quaint bridges and little gondolas."

"So that was why I sent David. He seemed to know what he was doing, and he said he wanted to revisit old haunts, as it were. It seemed to me that the other drivers just wanted to go for the cheap booze and fags."

Outside the office, Williams smiled rather smugly, and said "I think I'm beginning to get a pretty good idea what happened, now, eh? It's all beginning to fall into place nicely."

Brian Probert nodded noncommittally, "I'm going to have a chat with the other drivers."

"Waste of time," added Gerald Williams, but tagged along nevertheless.

The drivers presented as depressing an aspect as the coaches did. They were lounging in an even less salubrious old railway wagon (beside where the door should have been was a sign, "Rest Room").

They weren't able to add very much to the little already known. David Jenkins was a quiet sort, a bit of a Lothario. After Williams' prompting, the drivers said they didn't think he was very religious, but that he certainly didn't seem the sort to break any major laws. Although married, he was supposed to have a 'friend' in the village, but had no obvious money problems, other than a mortgage and two women with a liking for the big Primark store in Cardiff.

The choir secretary was Ifor Jenkins. "No relation, see."

Brian Probert asked how the holiday had gone.

"Well, we weren't too sure whether to use old Eli or not. Most of us had had bad experiences at one time or another with his old crates, but he assured us he'd be buying a new executive cruiser especially for us, and, well, he was much cheaper than anybody else. And I must say most of it went off pretty well. There were hardly any hitches at all, considering."

"Was there anything unusual that happened?" urged Probert.

"There were a few odd little things that happened," continued Ifor Jenkins. "There was a little altercation between the driver and the hotel reception when we arrived. David said they hadn't booked a room for him, although I'm sure they had, as I'd arranged that myself directly with the hotel. In the end, he said they'd arranged for him to move into a sister hotel a couple of hundred yards away, but that it wouldn't inconvenience us at all. And he kept his word: he always called around at breakfast time each day, and turned up well before time for the tours. But I and some of the other choristers felt that the problem had been orchestrated by David, so that he wouldn't have to stay with us in the same hotel."

Both detectives said "Mmmm."

"I mean, I'm sure we wouldn't have been an embarrassment to him." Unexpectedly, Ifor Jenkins let out a loud cackle. Both the detectives jumped.

"Then a few of my friends said they thought that they had seen him, or someone very like him, in Amsterdam with a woman: not a very attractive woman, rather cheap really, not very young, lots of make-up and cheap perfume, and that sort of thing. The first sighting was almost immediately after we had signed in at the hotel. But they weren't *sure* it was David."

Brian Probert thought, if the choir members had got close enough to smell the perfume, then they must surely have been able to recognise their driver as well. "Eli Jenkins said that David had told him he'd been to Amsterdam before. Perhaps he had met up with an old friend."

"That could be it," said Ifor Jenkins, nodding. "David didn't say that he'd been there before. He certainly didn't seem to know his way around. He got lost quite a lot, actually." He smiled, and the two detectives braced themselves for another strident laugh, but thankfully it never came.

"Then the Customs people searched our coach on the return. They didn't find anything, of course, but David looked a little, well, concerned when they asked him to open the driver's sleeping compartment, the one under the floor. I suppose that's for a spare driver to use, not that I can imagine old Eli ever paying for two drivers on one coach. Some of us thought that perhaps he had hidden some cigarettes there, or something like that. The Customs didn't find anything at all though. Oh, the Callaghans had too much whisky, but I don't think people worry about that these days, do they?"

He added thoughtfully, "They had quite a lot of watches too, but …"

"Anyway, the oddest thing was on the return journey. The Callaghans were quite concerned when the driver of an old car, a Ford Sierra they said, not only seemed to be taking an inordinate amount of interest in our coach, but actually followed us, at least from one of the M4 service areas, all the way back to Llandrofa."

"And …" Ifor Jenkins clearly relished leaving what he felt was the most dramatic element to last, "When Dolly and I were the last to leave the coach, there was an extra suitcase in the boot. It wasn't the one David had been using, and so I said I'd better take it as it obviously belonged to one of my people, but he insisted that it was company policy to return all lost property to their office. It wasn't like him to be so formal. Very strange."

"And was it one of the chorister's suitcases?" asked Brian Probert.

"I haven't had time to check," replied Ifor Jenkins. "It was only a couple of hours ago wasn't it?"

Outside Ifor Jenkins' house, Gerald Williams seemed quite pleased with himself. "Well, I think that that's probably all wrapped up now, eh? I think I'll pop into Caer and spend a few well-earned hours at my Club."

"I don't know," mused his colleague. "I thought I might pop into the town and have a chat with some of the locals at the Melin. I wouldn't mind trying to find out a little more about our friend David Jenkins' background."

Gerald Williams looked as if he thought it pointless, but brightened up, "Yes, yes, the more you find out about Jenkins' financial background, the more we'll understand his motives. Good idea. You don't mind doing it on your own, do you, only I've got some business to attend to in Caer … "

Back at the Station the next morning, the Superintendent was waiting expectantly.

"Case all neatly wrapped up, boys?" asked the Superintendent. He rubbed his hands together, but didn't really look that hopeful.

Gerald Williams grinned smugly, "Well, I know why the driver was killed, but we will probably never find out who did it … unless we get Interpol involved, that is … "

"Go on. Explain it all to me, boy," urged the Superintendent.

"Well, right from the start, the fact that the coach went to Amsterdam suggested … well, it did to me at least … that drugs could have been at the bottom of all this."

"And all the odd little things that occurred confirmed my theory. David Jenkins clearly went out of his way to make certain that he was in a separate hotel, obviously to give himself the privacy to conduct his illicit little deals. Then he was seen with a strange woman: unsuspecting dupes are often lured into bringing drugs into the country by becoming sexually involved with an unscrupulous woman in the employ of some drugs gang. Apart from his obvious distress when the Customs were taking a interest in his coach, there was one final damning clue: it was clearly a member of the gang who tailed the coach home in order to retrieve the suitcase, full of drugs, which had been planted in the coach."

"As a matter of fact," Williams continued pompously, "I have long been worried that drugs and other contraband could easily be imported into the U.K. by criminals putting suitcases containing drugs amongst the innocent luggage about to be loaded into a tourist coach abroad."

"Excellent," said the Superintendent. He acted slightly paternally towards Gerald

Williams, and seemed to be overly pleased that it was he who had formulated the theory. "If we get statements off all those involved, and send details to Interpol, then we can safely close the case at this end."

"Have you go anything to add, Probert?" the Superintendent asked.

"I can give you the name of the person who killed David Jenkins," Probert said quietly.

The Superintendent's mouth opened and shut wordlessly a few times, as if he were some hand puppet operated by a small child who hadn't quite got the hang of things yet. Then he regained his composure slightly to add, "Even so, there's not a lot we can do, except to pass on the data to Interpol in Amsterdam, eh?"

Probert continued, "Actually, he lives just down the road from here, Superintendent."

"Come on," said the Superintendent discouragingly, "It was obvious from the start, to some of us at least, that drugs were at the bottom of this case. You're not suggesting we have a major drugs problem here in Llandrofa, are you?"

Brian Probert shook his head, "No, I don't think so. Actually, I also considered the possibility of drug trafficking being involved at first, but it soon became clear that David Jenkins wasn't the type to be involved in misdemeanours of that sort. All the evidence that my colleague has given seemed as if it could to relate to some secret, possibly a crime, and possibly relating to drugs, but little of it seemed *consistent*, if you see what I mean."

"Certainly, some of what we found out about David Jenkins suggested that he intended to commit some crime or hide some secret. His insisting on accommodation separate from the rest of the coach party suggested from the very start a *premeditated* plan and a need for secrecy. And, in Amsterdam, most secrets seem to be related to drugs ... or to bizarre sex, but I gather David Jenkins was perfectly normal in that sense."

"His uncomfortable attitude at Customs, and his not wanting to relinquish the suitcase also suggested that he had some secret to hide. And of course the suitcase was never found, so someone must have taken that."

"And yet ... if he had been consciously smuggling drugs, why use something as obvious as a large suitcase, when smaller packets could easily have been hidden around the coach, or in the drivers' under-floor compartment? No, the extra suitcase has all the hallmarks of some gang having either introduced the additional suitcase into the pile waiting to be loaded outside the hotel, or having put it into the boot unnoticed. The drugs would then have been brought though Customs without David's knowledge."

"And this innocent dupe theory fits in with David having been seen with some woman almost immediately after the coach arrived in Amsterdam. The drugs dealers would need to obtain some information as to when the coach would be loaded for the return journey, and what the return route and itinerary would be. David would hardly have had time to form a relationship himself so soon after his arrival in Amsterdam."

Williams interrupted here, "But couldn't he have been meeting up with an old friend? Couldn't this woman have been an acquaintance from previous visits of his to Amsterdam? He might have been involved with drugs before, you know."

Probert shook his head. "I did a bit of checking. He never *had* been further than Boulogne in his life."

He continued, "Anyway, there's an awful lot of money to be made from drugs. Surely, a gang of drug-traffickers would have used a much younger and more attractive girl as a sure-fire lure when so much money was at stake?"

"So, if David Jenkins' crime was drug smuggling, half the evidence suggests that he had planned this from the start, whilst the rest suggests that he was an innocent carrier. It just doesn't add up."

"But the car was the most interesting aberration from my colleague's theories," Probert continued.

"Surely, if a drugs dealer either wished to collect a piece of luggage planted on an unsuspecting coach driver, or didn't trust a new recruit, he would use a newer, more reliable car, and wouldn't make his following the coach obvious even to a bunch of elderly church choristers?"

"No, we have to find the theory that best fits all the information we have."

"And you have one?" snarled the Superintendent.

"Well, yes, actually." Probert stretched his legs comfortably. "If all this business weren't connected with drugs, and David Jenkins had never been to Amsterdam before, then how did he become so friendly so quickly with this woman he was seen with? I went over this in my mind for a little while, and then the solution, one that fitted all the facts, gradually became clear."

"What if the woman seen with David Jenkins in Amsterdam had been his girlfriend from Llandrofa? It could have been her luggage over which he fought on the return to Llandrofa, and it would have been because of her that he wanted privacy in the other hotel. And the only way in which he would have been able to smuggle her into Holland without the choir's knowing would have been in the driver's compartment, which explains his unease at the Customs. However, David Jenkins being an honest sort and not wishing to be found out, he probably made a booking for her to board the ferry as a foot passenger, and rejoin the coach on the quay afterwards."

"So who was in the car that followed them from the motorway service area on the M4?" Williams asked.

"That was the girlfriend's husband," Probert explained. "He followed the coach until the driver dropped off his wife in the little lane below the village. There was then either a violent fight resulting in David's death, or else the husband merely ambushed and killed him."

"Some of the choir members should be able to identify both the husband and his car. He has an old Ford Sierra as a matter of interest. And his wife may be able to confirm that her husband returned home shortly after her, or she may even have actually witnessed David's death. You'll have to keep her husband away from her when you question her, though."

"So, do you want his name and address?" Probert smiled.

Interval

Mrs. Guiteras was still fussing over the food. Nigella thought that she was probably one of those people who love hosting parties and preparing meals of great originality and inventiveness, but who don't really like eating much themselves.

A large and verminous-looking cat wandered in from the garden. It looked too unkempt and dirty to belong to the Guiteras family, and Nigella hoped it would keep away from her.

She knew that quite a few of her fellow students were cat-lovers, but she herself was an ailurophobe. Naturally, the flea-ridden beast headed straight for her, and began to gently rub herself against her leg.

Julie Janes was next to read.

Julie was a tall, thin student who wore clothes that emphasised her rather gawky aspect. She was clearly the shyest of the group assembled there, and so the Professor felt her confidence would probably become less assured as the evening wore on, and that it would be as well for her to make her contribution towards the beginning of the evening.

Glass in hand, Julie stumbled to the front of the audience, sat down rather self-consciously, and began, "Well, I hope you don't mind, but I'm afraid my story is set in Wales, too. Um, I thought it would make it a little more exotic ..." Her voice trailed off apologetically, but then, after a considerable plundering of her wine glass, she seemed to gain a little confidence.

Her story began.

It was interrupted by frequent scratching noises emanating from Nigella's corner.

Cinéma Vérité

Dick Jones was lying on the sofa in his lounge, his body contorted into a hideously unnatural shape.

He was cutting his toenails. He was having particular difficulty in trying to cut the nail on the little toe of his left foot when his telephone rang.

In theory, mobile phones are a great convenience: you can carry them with you wherever you happen to go. In practice, *they* are never where *you* happen to be. The concept is very similar to that of the stopped clock: a stopped clock is exactly right twice a day, whereas a slow clock is rarely right. So with telephones: when an ordinary telephone rings, you *may* be right next to it, whereas, with a mobile phone, you are *never* right next to it.

By its sound, Dick Jones thought the phone was behind the sofa. After much futile searching, he finally found it deep within the sofa itself.

"Mr. Dick Jones?" a formal voice asked. Dick nodded, so the voice continued, "I have been given your name by a mutual friend, and I understand that you are a bit of a film buff." By his use of this last phrase, it was obvious the caller had not encountered it until very recently. "My name is Inspector Nurdin, and we are currently in the middle of conducting a murder enquiry." Inspector Nurdin unbended slightly to add, "The truth is that we're pretty sure we have the right man. In fact, he's the only suspect there is. But we were wondering whether you could pop down to the Station this afternoon, and help us with our enquiries …"

"The problem is," he continued, "He has the perfect watertight alibi."

"He says he was on his own in a cinema at the time of the murder."

All the way down in his car (having refused the offer to be picked up by a Police car at this house because of what the neighbours might think), Dick Jones was puzzling as to how being alone at a cinema could present the perfect alibi. If no-one could confirm his presence there, how could he use this to prove his innocence?

At the Police Station, he went up to the Desk Sergeant and asked where he could find Inspector Nurdin. He was escorted to a very small cupboard-like room at the back of the building with the Inspector's name prominently displayed on the door.

"Sorry to bother you. It's all quite unofficial of course," the Inspector volunteered, offering Dick a chair. "You probably know to which case I'm referring, anyway."

Dick did know, as there had been only one crime of any significance in the area in the last month or so.

"Yes, Julie Hopkins, a young girl from Cardiff, was murdered two days ago. She went to see her aunt in Swansea by bus the first Saturday of each month. So, the day before yesterday, she left her aunt's house around four o'clock to walk back to the shops and the bus station, and she was found dead, strangled, outside Aberdu Police Station just after ten p.m. The time of her death was between eight and when she was found. No-one appears to have seen her after four."

"Even after only a few hours' investigation, it emerged that there was only one real suspect, a Mr. Stuart Hawkins. He seems quite a clever lad. His father owns a string of shops and is pretty rich. It seems this Julie Hopkins went out with him for a while, but then he finished with her. She wasn't very happy about that. She was quite a pretty girl, and probably not used to being dumped … and, well, she had hinted to a few friends that she may have been pregnant."

"Anyway, even as we began to realise that he was a suspect, he turned up at the Station here to insist that he be kept under observation until we accepted his innocence. He's been in a cell here since then, just until we could sort it all out – well, we had the space – but now he's getting fed up and wants a decision out of us."

"He claims to have visited one of the cinemas in Cardiff city centre on his own that evening, and to have seen the whole of some new film 'PR3,' which was showing from eight to ten o'clock. We've checked the times. The point of all this is that it was the first time the film had ever been shown anywhere in the country. It had never been shown to the British public before."

"So he gave himself up, well, sort of, the next day. He realised, the same as we had, that, unless it was a random, motiveless killing, he was the only real suspect. He felt that his only alibi was to be able to prove that he was in Cardiff watching the film at the very time Julie was being murdered and dumped in Swansea. If he could prove he could remember the film all the way through, then he couldn't have murdered the girl."

"And, even with his flashy sports car, Aberdu is a good fifty minutes' drive from Cardiff."

"Could he have seen the film at a press session, or in America, or heard about it from a friend who had seen it?" Dick Jones asked.

"We thought of that," the Inspector replied, "But it was released in America on the same day. It was shown at a press session in London a few weeks ago, but he has a cast-iron alibi for that time, and so he couldn't have been there in person. And he doesn't seem to have any acquaintances who might have seen it then. And he doesn't know anybody in the film industry. Either way, he seems to have first-hand knowledge of almost the entire film."

"So what do you want me to do?" asked Dick.

"Well, the distribution company has kindly lent us a copy of the film. It's quite good, actually: all the lads at the Station have seen it."

"We've watched the film over and over again, and asked Hawkins questions ad nauseam about it. He doesn't remember every small detail about the film of course. When I watch a film, I try to enjoy it, and I certainly don't remember all the car registration numbers and other trivia like that. But he seems to recall most of the important things, even the visual elements, for almost the whole length of the film. He remembers the colour of the villain's car, the sort of dog the hero's girlfriend has, and that sort of thing. He says he popped out to the lavatory for about ten minutes at one point around the middle of the film, but that hardly gives him time to drive to Swansea and murder someone."

"He's still amenable enough, but we'll have to release him soon. You have a lot of knowledge about films. What we'd like you to do, as a last resort more or less, is to have a chat with him after seeing the film - for free, of course – and then let us know whether you think he saw the film that night or not."

"It's as simple as that," Inspector Nurdin said, standing up. "If we can't find any reason to doubt that he saw the film between eight and ten that evening, it means that he can't have killed that poor girl, and we'll have to let him go."

"See what you think," were his parting words, as he escorted Dick into the makeshift cinema to view the film.

Stuart Hawkins was sitting in his cell fairly happily. The door was clearly unlocked, on the assumption that he would be rather stupid to leave until the Police were willing to accept his alibi. He also had as many creature comforts as the Force felt were permissible and affordable. However, he was clearly bored and wanting to leave as soon as possible.

"Are you the last one?" he asked as Dick Jones entered the cell. "Quite honestly, I'm getting a little fed up here, but I'm not leaving until all of you admit that I couldn't have killed her."

Dick had already seen the film a couple of times, and had noted down a few points that he thought he might use to decide whether Hawkins had actually seen the film, or had had it described to him by someone else.

"Actually, it's quite a good film, isn't it?" Dick Jones began. Hawkins grunted dismissively. "Look, do you mind if I try and sort this all out by asking you a few questions about the film?"

"O.K., but I had to pop to the loo just after the sex scene on the train. I mean, I couldn't go in the middle of that, could I? So I lost about ten minutes of the film at that point. I probably shouldn't have visited that Indian restaurant lunchtime. Inspector Nurdin has probably told you he checked with the restaurant about that."

Dick nodded absent-mindedly. "Right," he started. He was trying to act in a friendly manner, but, not being a member of the police force, realised that he probably felt as uneasy and uncomfortable there as Hawkins did. "What colour was the dress Jackie Grant took off before the sex scene?"

"It was orange ... and it was a trouser suit."

"In what time of the year were the opening shots set?"

"There were no leaves on the trees in the park, so it must have been autumn or winter."

"What sort of car did Crispin Goole drive?"

"Lotus ... Elan perhaps, an old model ... light blue ... CKN 9 or something?"

"What was the first thing that Goole did on entering his flat?"

"After the fight with the bald man, or with Jackie Grant after visiting her grandmother? Oh, it doesn't matter, I'll tell you what happened both times. The first time, after the fight, he lay down and she fetched him a whisky, in a tall glass, with ice, which he contemptuously threw into a corner of the room. The second time, they made love halfway up the stairs. He lived in a mews cottage, not a flat anyway."

After about an hour of this quizzing (he hardly felt it could be called grilling), Dick Jones left Hawkins' cell, and returned to the makeshift cinema. He sat and thought for a while.

It was about ten minutes later that Inspector Nurdin entered the little room and interrupted his thoughts. "Have you got anywhere with Hawkins?" he asked. His voice sounded resigned to disappointment.

Dick Jones looked up, as if waking from a short nap. "Oh, I'm absolutely convinced he saw the film that night. All the way through, too, from eight to ten o'clock, except for that loo visit."

"That's it, then, I suppose," mused the Inspector. "Thanks for your help, but I suppose we'll have to let him go. He can't have driven all the way from Cardiff to Aberdu and back in ten minutes."

"No," continued Dick Jones, "But it's enough time to persuade a young girl to accompany you into the men's toilet, strangle her, and then drop her out of the window into a convenient lane below."

The Inspector looked confused. "But the cinema's in Cardiff and the body was found in Aberdu."

"It may have been the first time the film was shown to the public anywhere in the U.K., but I'm pretty certain it was also shown in a lot of other cities too. You can check, but I think you'll find it was showing in Swansea as well. Hawkins must have known Julie's habits pretty well. He could have driven to Swansea that afternoon, and then casually picked her up on her way back from her aunt's. If he had suggested starting up their relationship again, I'm sure she would have agreed to his taking her to the cinema in Swansea. I can think of a number of reasons why she might agree to go with him into the toilet, especially after that sex scene in the film. Once there, he could have strangled her in a cubicle, and dumped her body through the window. You'll have to check up on the convenience of such a window and whether there was easy access below, of course. It's only a few minutes' drive to Aberdu from the centre of Swansea, and he's got a fast car. And dumping her body outside the police station is a very good way of fixing the times for his alibi. "

"Yes, yes. And he was rather late in getting home that night, I gather. How can we prove it?" asked Inspector Nurdin thoughtfully.

"You could start by asking patrons and staff at the cinema in Swansea if they recognise Hawkins. They probably wouldn't, though. But you could also check with the staff of both cinemas if anything unusual happened that night, and see whether Hawkins remembered it."

"But your best bet is to ask him about the advertisements or trailers they showed. The days of 'Why not visit the Kalahari Restaurant, only five minutes from this cinema' may be gone, but there should be something different about the two showings in Cardiff and Swansea."

"And someone in Swansea may remember seeing a man and a young girl in a rather flashy sports car."

"Thank you," said Inspector Nurdin. "I'm glad we sorted it out."

"None of us here liked the little creep anyway."

Interval

Some of the others had started scratching now.

Thankfully, they were all able to move about a little now, as Professor Guiteras announced that the food was finally ready.

Nigella was pleased: not a sausage roll or a bit-of-pineapple-and-cheese-on-a-stick was to be seen. The buffet seemed to be a combination of good basic English food and Spanish tapas. Cold meats and salads abounded, as did fish and other seafood. The peacock in the centre turned out to be a ham with slices of kiwi fruit for the 'eye' feathers.

The wine was equally good, but not something to be rushed. The Professor had obviously decided to have a cold buffet so that the meal could be returned to as often as possible, rather in the way that the French have a course every thirty minutes or so, interspersed with dancing or chatting or, knowing the French, whatever.

Therefore, after what seemed only a couple of minutes, the host called upon Luke Williams to continue the entertainment.

Luke looked up from his plate (china, not paper, was unusual in student circles, Nigella thought). He looked rather shocked. After a few seconds, he got rather unsteadily to his feet and moved into the arena.

On the Warpath

Miss Murgatroyd looked at her watch. "Up Your Garden Path," with her favourite gardening presenter, Matt Wetherall, would be on in ten minutes. That left just enough time for her to finish weeding under the hedge, tidy up her gardening tools, make a (quick) cup of tea, and put her feet up in front of the television.

And then something very unusual happened.

Her next door neighbour, Mrs. Betty Wright, never received friends, indeed appeared not to have any at all. Apart from when out shopping, and then very occasionally, she never seemed to meet anyone, and had little time for conversation even with her neighbours. She had three children, two boys, one girl, all married, none with children, but only saw them briefly at birthdays (sometimes) and Christmas (with a different family each year, and not staying overnight): she didn't like any of them very much, she once professed. Her husband had died twenty years previously, and she had devoted herself to her garden ever since.

And so it was fairly unusual that footsteps could be distinctly heard coming up Mrs. Wright's path. Miss Murgatroyd couldn't see through the hedge, but her hearing was very acute.

But what was *very* unusual was Mrs. Wight's voice: it sounded surprised, perhaps almost shocked, but it sounded as if she were actually pleased to see her visitor. "Hello. It is you, isn't it? But, but, you can't be here *now*!"

After a brief pause, Mrs. Wright appeared to collect herself, and purred happily, "You must come in for a cup of tea and some cake. I can't tell you what a shock it was seeing you then - but it was a *very* pleasant one. On Wednesday evening, too!"

Miss Murgatroyd recovered from her surprise sufficiently to put away her tools and return indoors to watch her favourite television programme. Her weeding remained unfinished.

Mrs. Wright's lounge (or would she call it a parlour?) was neat and tidy and ostentatiously well-dusted. It gave the impression that there was another room somewhere at the back of the small cottage where anything that 'didn't fit in' was consigned, but in fact she didn't possess anything that 'didn't fit in.' In the centre of the room was a small table with two tea-cups, now empty, a sugar bowl, an ornate milk jug, and one of those strange multi-tiered porcelain cake stands on which resided a slab of supermarket Battenberg cake, partially-sliced, but not consumed.

The only untidy element in the whole room, Inspector Jacks thought, was Mrs. Wright herself. She was lying beside the table in a most asymmetric position. A small log had been carefully replaced amongst the others in the fireplace, but was clearly covered in blood.

Miss Murgatroyd had been asked in to unofficially identify the body, and to say what she knew of Mrs. Wright's last hours. She recounted what she had heard the previous evening in the garden.

"So it must have been someone she knew well, someone she particularly liked, and someone she trusted, eh?" Inspector Jacks added, thoughtfully.

"But that's the point," blurted out Miss Murgatroyd. "She hardly knew anyone apart from her children. She didn't like anyone, especially her children. She had no grandchildren. And I don't think she's trusted anyone since Leslie died."

"I'm sure it's all to do with that letter," she said finally. "Do you want me to look for it?"

With the Inspector's permission, Miss Murgatroyd hunted around a bit, and eventually found it in a drawer in the sideboard. She handed the letter to Inspector Jacks.

She continued, "One reason why the children never bothered her much is that they didn't think she was worth anything. She only had the house, but they had that valued when she was ill ten years ago - the children thought they might have to put her into a home - and they found it was worth hardly anything at all. Apart from its having no central heating or double-glazing, and the kitchen and bathroom being in urgent need of renovation, there were problems with cracks in the walls and damp. I don't know what underpinning is, but they thought the house might need that."

"But that didn't worry these 'Heroes of Gardening' people. They offered her a huge sum for the house because the gardens were originally landscaped years ago by George Mutton ... or a name like that anyway. They didn't seem worried about the condition of the house. But the offer was only until the end of this month."

Inspector Jacks unfolded the letter. It had 'Heroes of Gardening' across the top in bold letters. Below that were the names of the ten directors: a few were Sirs, one or two were acknowledged gardening experts, one was a learned historian, but almost all had long strings of letters after their names. The first paragraph introduced the Society, and said its stated aim was to preserve for future generations gardens of especial interest to flower-lovers, both because of their particular qualities and because of their associations with famous horticulturists of the past. There was a list of properties already acquired and now opened to the public 'at reasonable cost.' The second paragraph made a most tempting offer, whilst the third gave the number of a contact with whom she could get in touch if she wished to take advantage of the offer, but with "an absolute" deadline of the end of the month.

"Mrs. Wright didn't want to accept the offer?" Inspector Jacks asked.

"Well, she *was* interested at the beginning. She confided to me over the azaleas one day - a very rare occurrence - that she rather liked the idea of her garden and the result of her work there being preserved for all time. But then she found out that they intended to demolish everything that she had done there and restore it to the layout when Mutton owned it. They had got hold of some old photographs, I gather."

"Mmm … So it could be that someone murdered her to get control of the house, before it plummeted back to its real value. The three children were her only beneficiaries, I suppose." The Inspector was a great believer in the verity of information gained from unofficial sources.

Miss Murgatroyd had been thinking of that too.

"Yes," she said, "But I don't think she would ever have welcomed any of her children in such a friendly way as she did last night."

By Friday morning, Patcham Police had verified all that Miss Murgatroyd had said, and had interviewed Mrs. Wright's three children, all of whom had the usual not-quite-watertight alibi that they were at home with their respective spouses. The forensic department had found quite a lot of evidence at the scene, too, but none of it could be matched against those likely to inherit.

There was one additional point of interest. Miss Murgatroyd said that Mrs Wright went out shopping every Wednesday and Saturday. She said she had set out as usual this Wednesday. She always boarded the 69A bus to Patcham at one thirty.

But the driver said she had failed to catch his bus this week. None of the other drivers on that route had seen her either. The staff at her usual supermarket had missed her too.

The next few days involved very little creative deduction, merely a large number of police persons interviewing bus drivers, taxi drivers, and the staff at most of the local shopping centres.

Eventually, it emerged that Mrs. Wright had boarded a bus at about the same time, but travelling in the opposite direction. She had alighted at Sichley, ten miles away. A few pedestrians thought that they *might* have seen her, but none of them were sure. Certainly, no shop staff remembered her.

However, the Inspector's luck seemed to be improving, when, chatting casually with Miss Murgatroyd during one of his occasional visits to her late neighbour's house, he mentioned Sichley. "Her solicitor has his office there, you know," she mused.

Considering the fact that they had hardly ever spoken very much, Miss Murgatroyd appeared to have an almost encyclopaedic knowledge of her neighbour's way of life.

Triumphantly, with what he hoped was the one last vital piece of information almost in his grasp, Inspector Jacks mounted the stairs to a little office in a rundown building off Sichley High Road. 'Freeman, Hardy & O'Grady' were at the very top of the creaking building.

Inspector Jacks was shown into the main, and only, office off the small reception area. The sole proprietor was a Mr. Willis. For a country solicitor, he seemed a rather shady character.

Inspector Jacks showed his credentials, and briefly stated his reason for visiting, as Mr. Willis was clearly agitated by his presence.

He decided to sound rather more confident and sure than he actually was. "I understand one of your clients, a Mrs. Wright, visited you last Wednesday afternoon. I require to know whether it was in connection with her will, or perhaps with some problem that was worrying her."

"Nope," replied Mr. Willis, "Haven't seen her for yonks. I was here all last Wednesday, er, talking with another client, and she didn't call in, or try to make an appointment." He pressed the only button on his intercom, and asked, "You didn't meet Mrs. Wright last Wednesday did you, Sharon? No? She didn't call in and ask to see me when I was busy, did she? No?"

"That's it, Chief. No-one here saw her. She didn't come near us."

It was now a week since Mrs. Wright's demise, and Inspector Jacks still had no idea at all who could have called on her that fatal night. It would perhaps have been better if his problem were that he had such a long list of possible suspects that it was difficult to whittle down this number, but in fact he had few candidates, none of whom seemed really eligible.

He decided to call upon Miss Murgatroyd, as it were, on the anniversary of the murder.

"You've not called at the best of times, Inspector," said Miss Murgatroyd, still trying to get around to finishing her work under the hedge. "I'm afraid our favourite gardening programme is on tonight, and we all watch it religiously. We can have a little chat when it's over, if you like. It's only half-an-hour."

Inspector Jacks' heart sank. He hated gardening, gardeners, gardens in general, and gardening programmes in particular, and he currently felt particularly strongly against all things horticultural, immersed as he was in what he saw as an extremely perplexing case. But he clearly had no option if he wanted to talk to Miss Murgatroyd. He certainly didn't fancy returning to the station, and coming back at another time.

He followed the old lady into her lounge. She motioned him silently to a seat, and then she positioned herself in what was obviously *her* armchair, set right in front of the television. On a small table alongside were a copy of the 'Radio Times,' a half-finished cup of tea, and a small arsenal of spectacles. Rather than risk missing the first few moments of the programme, Miss Murgatroyd had switched on a little too early. The Inspector had to endure not only the titles of the preceding programme, but also the adverts., and so had plenty of time to think about the case.

Apart from the possibly-important question of where Mrs. Wright had visited on the afternoon of her death, the main problem, or so it seemed to Inspector Jacks, was why Mrs. Wright was so friendly and accommodating to her visitor, when she apparently had no friends or relatives, or indeed anyone she really liked at all.

"Did Mrs. Wright watch this programme as well?" he asked, trying to make conversation.

Miss Murgatroyd nodded distractedly. It was obvious she did not expect him to talk until the half-hour was over, but, suddenly, the theme music of "Up Your Garden Path" began. Miss Murgatroyd put a commanding finger to her lips, and sank bank into her armchair.

The puerile music seemed to consist of some half-remembered rustic ballad overlaid with an irritating drum rhythm.

When the titles were over, Inspector Jacks found himself looking at a too-handsome presenter, clearly overdressed for gardening, discussing the best way to cultivate dahlias in a chalky soil.

Miss Murgatroyd was clearly captivated, but Inspector Jacks found his patronising attitude difficult to bear. He also suspected that the presenter probably knew as little about gardening as he, and might even share his dislike of the pastime. But the old lady had a dreamy expression on her face, and, if the thought as to whether or not he actually had any horticultural knowledge or abilities had ever crossed her mind, it obviously did not worry her either way. During the half-hour, she only spoke once, when a nubile blonde girl appeared to assist him in selecting flowers with complementary colours. "Pah! That Candy Celandine. What does she know about gardening?"

At the end of the programme, the presenter announced that he hoped that his dear viewers had enjoyed the half-hour as much as he, and that his name was Matt Wetherall.

Inspector Jacks realised that he had seen the name somewhere before.

But where?

It took him a few moments to recollect.

When he remembered that it had been amongst the list of directors on the letter from 'Heroes of Gardening,' he realised that, for the last thirty minutes, he had been watching Mrs. Wright's murderer.

Matt Wetherall was as insincere in life as he was on television. On being interviewed by the Police regarding Mrs. Wright's death, his originally-gentle television manner suddenly changed to reveal a more violent nature.

Eventually, he admitted that George Mutton had been one of his ancestors, and that the acquisition of Mrs. Wright's house had been a personal project of his. But he still denied having called to see the old lady at any time.

The forensic department was able to prove otherwise, and Matt Wetherall was tried and found guilty of the murder of Mrs. Wright.

Inspector Jacks could imagine his calling on poor old Mrs. Wright that Wednesday, expecting to win her over with his oft-used and insincere charms. As others had, he would have expected her to accept anything he might ask of her, but she had failed to succumb to his charisma. It would have been one of the first times in his life that he had failed to get what he wanted, and her refusal must have severely damaged his self-esteem.

Many colleagues and acquaintances had confirmed that a more violent side of his personality was never very far below the surface of the urbane air he projected on television ...

Despite his gratification at having solved the murder, Inspector Jacks was still puzzled over one point. As he confided to a colleague in 'The Rose and Anchor,' "What we can't understand is where the old dear went to on the afternoon she was killed."

The new tenants moved into Mrs. Wright's old house.

Amongst the once-prized articles and junk they threw out were three small garden gnomes found in the shed at the bottom of the garden. They were marked, "Matt Wetherall's Country Garden Range," and, underneath in large red letters, "Three for the Price of Two! Another Great Offer from Berkeley's of Sichley."

Interval

Sally Rush was next.

The Milk of Human Unkindness

It was a bright cold day in April, and the digital clock on the tower of Marche Barrington Town Hall was showing 13:00.

And still there had been no refuse collection in Gobelow Lane.

Gobelow Lane was a fairly long road that ran westwards from the market square of Marche Barrington, past the local parish church and cemetery (which local historians had for long argued over as the source of the strange name of the road), and on towards Dithersham. The road started as a quaint narrow little lane, which had only been made adequately wide for vehicular traffic by the removal of the small front gardens of the first few buildings. This was the old part of the lane, as shown by the once-graceful Georgian facades of these houses, all now unsympathetically converted into shops, bars and restaurants. The road widened considerably afterwards, as the remainder of the lane had been developed only in the past few years or so. The houses here had been built at some distance from the road, and were all "architecturally-designed" (which leaves one wondering who it is that designs other houses). Even if these houses looked very expensive by modern standards, they still failed to convey the same style as their more elderly neighbours once had.

There was a small knot of people gathered close to, but not *too* close to, the area of the Lane where it widened. The onlookers would probably have liked to have moved closer, but were prevented by a highly-developed sense of propriety and decency, as well as a police barrier.

Kitty Huggett was a fairly reasonable witness, Sergeant Sharp thought. She seemed sensible and was fairly lucid, but it helped if you ignored every other sentence.

"Well, myself and my sister Mary were walking back to the village - we still call it a village even though it's a lot bigger now, of course - and we saw Mr. Galsworthy putting his rubbish bags out. We know him, knew him, from when he called into the shop for his tobacco some Sunday mornings."

"Anyway, he always takes a while to put the bags out. He always does it so carefully, putting them where the dogs and children can't get at them. Sometimes, you know, you can have all your *private* rubbish strewn all across the road."

"We often seem to be passing around that time of the week, so we know he's usually there for a while. I think he's a solicitor or a barrister or an accountant or something like that. Anyway, he's always very precise, and the bags are always set out in tidy little rows along the wall. Mary says they're like little soldiers standing there."

"Well, we'd almost drawn level with Mr. Galsworthy, and we were looking into the trees opposite where there were some little birds, you know the pretty little ones in that advertisement for the retirement pension scheme, when we heard a squeal of brakes. There was one of those huge milk tankers that had just passed along the narrow part of the road. I don't know why they can't find another route: they always seem to be up and down our lane. Anyway, the driver didn't seem to have been going that fast, but a little girl ran out from a lane by the side of the last old house - it's now a bar or a bistro or something like that - and the driver had to swerve quite sharply to avoid her."

"It wasn't the driver's fault. Mr. Galsworthy just happened to be beside the wall, tending to his rubbish bags, and well ..."

"We all rushed across to see if Mr. Galsworthy were all right, but we couldn't tell because he was under one of the wheels."

"The driver reversed his tanker a little, and we could see Mr. Galsworthy was still breathing slightly."

Sergeant Sharp asked, "Did he say anything?"

"Well, he said something like "Ah, that's better," and then he just seem to faint away."

"The driver of the tanker didn't have a telephone in his cab, but one of our neighbours called for an ambulance. I gather he died on the way to the Hospital. I don't know what happened to the little girl, as I didn't see her afterwards. I imagine if one of her parents had been there they would have rushed her away pretty quickly."

Sergeant Sharp sighed fairly happily. What Miss Huggett had said agreed almost exactly with what all the other witnesses had said. It seemed fairly obvious that the incident was indeed an unfortunate accident, and the matter was closed.

And the matter would have remained closed, had one of Mr. Eliot Galsworthy's two other partners not been killed almost exactly a week later, run over by a milk tanker from the same company, driven by a fairly close relative of the first driver.

George Mills had worked for Milk! for around ten years, not that the firm had been called that for long. The Marche Barrington, Dithersham and District Milk and Dairy Products Co-operative had been formed in 1919 by three local men who had returned from the War with rather more ambition than money. The company had been started on land on the family farms but had never prospered much until a later and more dynamic generation had taken over in the early sixties and changed the name to the Milk Marche Board. Despite almost continuous threats of litigation and financial problems, they had made it through to the next generation, who had recently changed the name again to its present title. The company now had over sixty tankers, all based at the original farm site, and Milk! was the area's largest employer.

George was invited to the Police Station.

"Look, it just has to be a coincidence that Arthur was involved in that accident last week. I've got at least seven or eight other relatives working at the Depot. The Management likes personal recommendations."

Will Sharp nodded, "What exactly happened yesterday evening?"

"I'd just done all my deliveries around Ordernshire, and so I returned south along the Dithersham to Marche Barrington road. I reached Hellhag Cross just as it was getting dark - I could see well enough, mind you - and turned right onto the road to the Depot."

"After I went around the first corner by Poacher's Cottage - I remember I had to overtake a little white van, so I certainly couldn't have been going fast - there was a fairly straight stretch for about half-a-mile or so."

"A few yards past the Cottage, there's a small clump of trees on the left." He had been about to say 'copse' but thought that might have been taken disrespectfully. "Suddenly this elderly gentleman - I remember he seemed very thin and frail - appeared from behind one of the trees that overhangs the road, bounded over the ditch, and ran straight in front of my tanker. It was only later that I found out it was Mr. Dickens."

"I must have been more shocked than he was: well, he *was* dead, wasn't he? I got out to check, but there were certainly no signs of life. I ran back to Poacher's Cottage, old Cain's place, and asked if I could use his telephone - he's got one now - but he wouldn't let me in, so I had to yell into the phone through the letter-box. I don't blame people being like that, these days."

"And look, I'm not daft. I know all this seems wrong. Why would an old gent be hiding behind a tree in the middle of the country, far from his own house? He seemed pretty old, and yet he jumped over that stream pretty easily."

"And you've only got my word for it, as there wasn't anybody else about. Old Cain was in his cottage, and it was only well after the accident that I saw a fisherman loading his rods and lines into the van I'd overtaken, so I don't think he would have seen anything."

Will Sharp nodded. He'd already spoken on the phone to old Cain, who'd been unable to add anything, but he'd try and trace the fisherman, not that he'd expect much from him either.

Will Sharp was in the D.C.I.'s office.

"So what have we got? A death that must have been an accident, and some elderly gentleman leaping around the country like a young gazelle and throwing himself under the wheels of a milk tanker. I'd like to close the two cases, but the coincidence is too high."

"Young Simpson's been to see," the D.C.I. consulted his notes, "Mike Grady of Milk! He doesn't know anything, and can't think of any reason why his company should be involved in these deaths. He reckons there's nothing suspicious going on in his company. You never know, though."

"You'd better go and see Bennett Schwarz."

Miss Huggett had been right when she spoke so vaguely about Mr. Galsworthy's profession. The plaque outside the office merely said 'Galsworthy, Dickens, and Schwarz - Finance.' Sharp would have called around to see Bennett Schwarz as soon as he could anyway, but he received an urgent phone call from him as soon as he got into work that morning. Bennett Schwarz was clearly a very worried man.

"What exactly *do* you do?" asked Sharp.

"Ah," Bennett Schwarz said expansively, "Loans, property investment, et cetera, et cetera. Basically, if it's to do with money, and we think we can make a profit, then we're interested!" Bennett Schwarz smiled as if he'd made a particularly good joke.

"And if it's legal, I assume" added Sergeant Sharp.

Bennett Schwarz looked a little blank, before continuing, "But I suppose you want me to say if there's anyone who would hold a grudge against us?"

Sharp nodded and felt almost superfluous. "I think it would have to be a fairly serious grudge," he smiled.

"Mmm, well most of our dealings are with the larger institutions in London and the other financial capitals, and I wouldn't have thought they would have done anything like this ... if it is murder, of course. We certainly wouldn't deal with anybody who appeared to act outside the Law ... well, not often, anyway." He offered a smile, but this was quickly withdrawn.

"Let's see. We have varying degrees of financial involvement in most of the local companies, especially the larger ones. You do realise that many years ago we gained a controlling interest in the Marche Barrington Milk Company, or whatever they call themselves now, don't you?"

Sharp didn't. "Oh God," he said quietly.

He continued, "What about smaller investors, tenants, that sort of thing? To put it simply, has your firm upset anyone of late?"

"Well, I'm sure that, in the course of our activities over the years, we must have attracted the dislike of some people. That's inevitable with money and finance, isn't it? But there's been nothing recently of an unpleasant nature, I'm sure."

Mike Barnes at the Marche Gazette disagreed.

"Hell, no, they've been kicking people out of their houses and conducting dodgy deals for decades, and they're still doing it. They were particularly bad in the sixties and early seventies, when they were buying up properties and forcing the owners and tenants out onto the streets. It was all done just within the law though, or at least nobody could afford to challenge them."

"But in the last twenty years or so they've concentrated more on larger deals, and so they've probably become more responsible ... I mean, you don't rough up the big financial institutions."

"However, I do recall a few cases in the last few years or so that might fit the bill ..."

It was in the previous year that four elderly residents had been evicted from their rest home to make way for an "exciting new waterside development shopping arcade and pleasure mall."

The first contact was a Simon Ball. His stepmother was one of the four evicted.

"Actually, I don't know very much about her, believe it or not. My real mother died about thirty years ago. I don't think she really liked or approved of my father's profession. He was an impresario and theatre-owner. When she died, he threw himself into his work, and soon married a French actress and entertainer. She wasn't a straight theatrical actress. I think she worked more in variety or the circus or something. All I really know is that she was born Maria Legrand - I needed that for some forms - and my father said she took her stage surname from some French city because it rhymed. Anyway, she was Maria Ball when she moved into the home when my father died."

"As far as I knew, I was the only relative she had. I tried my best to fight against the eviction, if that's what you call it. I mean, everything was fully paid up, so I don't know how they got her and the others out. Anyway, despite being in her mid-seventies and very very frail, she elected to return to France, although I'm certain she didn't have any family there, and I did hear that she died a few weeks ago. No, I didn't go to her funeral. It was quite a long way away, you know."

Paul Radford was now living with his son and his family in a semi-detached in Croydon.

"My son was very upset when I became, shall we say, homeless, but I've certainly got no complaints. He and his wife were more or less forced to take me in, which is what I'd wanted all along. Ron was terrified I'd be recommended to go into a home where they'd take all my life savings to pay for my upkeep. Ha, he's not getting them anyway, as I've willed them to his kids. Not that they're much good to anyone."

"And no, he isn't the sort to murder anyone. Nor is his wife. Take my word for it." He winked.

Gordon Bennett was living on a barge moored on a tributary of the Thames.

"Been dying to try this all my life, actually. Being kicked out really gave me the impetus to do what I'd always wanted to do. If it'd happened twenty years earlier, I'd probably have backpacked around Europe like some damned student, but my leg's a bit of a problem now."

He tapped his leg. It sounded hollow.

Enid Byrne clearly had not got a hollow leg.

Her daughter also lived in a semi-detached in Croydon.

"The last I heard from her, she was backpacking around Greece, in Crete or Corfu or Rhodes or somewhere, island-shopping, I think she said."

She hunted around in a drawer, and then pounced on a post-card triumphantly. "Look, I said it was Greece. I've got a post-card dated last month from her in Ibiza."

It was six o'clock on Sunday morning, and Will Sharp was lying in bed thinking about the case. He still woke up at this time every Sunday morning. Since the children had been born, it was the only time he and his wife could be together, and he couldn't get out of the habit even though she now had a largely non-existent interest in such matters.

If the death of Eliot Galsworthy *had* been murder, how could it have been done? Surely no-one would send a child, or even a midget (he thought briefly of Maria Legrand's theatrical background) out right into the path of a heavy lorry? Unless, he thought, the driver were expecting it.

What if the child / midget had had a mobile phone to tell the driver when Galsworthy was putting out his litter, knowing he usually took some time to arrange the bags. The driver could start off from wherever he were parked, drive along Gobelow Lane, swerve when the child / midget appeared, and then run into old Galsworthy.

Was that plausible?

In that case, the whole business probably was connected in some way with the milk company ... or perhaps just with some of its drivers. But they had checked, and found no financial irregularities or scams within the company, and they could find no personal reasons for the two drivers bearing any sort of grudge against Galsworthy's finance company.

But if the first death *were* a very well-planned and executed murder, why was the second so badly planned?

Not only was it suspicious that a second partner had been killed so soon afterwards by a tanker from the same company - AND driven by a relative - but there were no independent witnesses, and the driver's testimony was distinctly odd, as he himself admitted.

And some of these implausibilities could have been removed so easily just by the driver's lying! Why did he say that Dickens leapt over the ditch with such ease? Why not just say that he walked out from the side of the road, or from behind the van the driver said he saw earlier? Why not make up a few fake bystanders to try to confuse the matter and suggest someone may have pushed him under the wheels?

Or were the two deaths unconnected? Might someone have decided to get rid of Mr. Dickens conveniently soon after the death of Mr. Galsworthy to suggest a link?

Sharp's thoughts seemed to be beginning to go round in circles when the telephone rang. He checked the time. It was now seven thirty. It was his superior officer, Derek Hughes.

"It's the final chapter, old boy. Bennett Schwarz has just received a phone call from someone at the milk company. They said they had information about the deaths and some sort of crime going on at the milk depot, and asked Schwarz to meet them there at nine. I'll pick you up in ten minutes."

Schwarz had, of course, been under constant guard and surveillance since the deaths, but the D.C.I. had given instructions that Hughes was to be contacted personally if any developments occurred, and so now he was taking over.

It was twenty minutes before Hughes appeared, and a further ten minutes before they reached Schwarz's mansion.

They still had about half-an-hour or so before setting off for the depot.

"What did the caller actually say? Did you recognise the voice, or did he have any sort of accent?" Sharp enquired.

Schwarz appeared rather stiff and preoccupied. "He just mentioned my partners' murders, and said there was something going on at the depot, and that I'd better come and have a look. I didn't recognise the voice, but I think he was trying to disguise it. It sounded false, almost like a combination of accents."

They sat and thought for a while, and then started off for the milk depot. Schwarz went in front in a car that was clearly almost brand-new: it was Japanese, but the manufacturer had sought to disguise its oriental mass-produced origins by omitting the company name altogether, and instead using a more upper-class mock English name as its marque. The policemen followed in their unmarked Mondeo.

Sharp looked disapprovingly at the car. "Huh, look, it's almost brand-new, and he's already scratched the door panel and lost the petrol filler cover." He snorted loudly.

It was a fairly boring journey to the depot, and so Will Sharp settled down in the passenger seat, relaxed, and resumed his analysis of the case now that additional information was available.

So, the whole matter was connected with the milk company after all. And murder *was* involved!

He started to go over all the things he had been thinking about in bed that morning. His thoughts were still going around in circles.

Was there anything that could fit in with all the facts and explain it all?

He decided to try and apply some lateral thinking.

After a while, he began to think that, actually, perhaps there was a suitable explanation. But surely what he was thinking was just too fantastic?

Was there anything that could corroborate his idea, even to a small degree?

The words of Simon Ball came back to him. They were so pleasantly cryptic that he had stored them at the back of his mind to play around with later.

"She took her stage surname from some French city because it rhymed."

What rhymed with Maria? Was there a French city called Baria ... or Caria ... or Daria? He went through all the alphabet without much success, not that he was very knowledgeable about French cities.

He began thinking back over his original fantastic theory. Suddenly he sat up in his seat.

Was there a French city that rhymed with 'ettes'?

Bettes, Cettes, Dettes ... again he went through the alphabet.

Metz was a French city.

Metz was a French city, and it rhymed.

METZ WAS A FRENCH CITY, AND IT RHYMED.

He though for a second or two, and then yelled "Stop him, stop him!"

Hughes looked surprised at the outburst, "Don't worry. We'll be at the depot in two minutes."

"It's got nothing to do with the milk company. I don't think he'll ever reach the depot."

His voice was sufficiently urgent to convince Hughes. "O.K. I'll pull him over after we've passed this van."

Sharp paled, "No, no, stop him now, NOW!"

Hughes flashed his headlights to get Schwarz's attention. But perhaps that was not the best idea under the circumstances. Because of the parked blue van, the road was effectively narrower here, and distracting Schwarz from the road ahead could have contributed considerably to his death.

It all happened very quickly.

Schwarz looked in his rear-view mirror to see why the Mondeo's headlights were flashing. At almost exactly the same time, something like a tree branch swung out from behind the van and caught his attention ... and then a little old lady walked slowly into the path of his car.

She appeared to be keeping to the side of the van and not crossing the road, so he only slowed slightly and moved a little towards the nearside of the road, away from her.

Suddenly, the old lady swung out a pram, and started pushing it right into his path. Schwarz braked and swung to the left, up onto the narrow pavement, but the impact with the kerb made him lose control, and the car dropped into the ditch at the side of the road.

"Christ," muttered Hughes.

"He should be O.K. He wasn't going that fast," said Sharp, hopefully.

But they had reckoned without the missing filler cover (and a missing filler cap they hadn't noticed). Petrol started pouring out onto grass that was already liberally soaked in petrol.

Something flew through the air, although the two policemen weren't sure whether it was from the little old lady or from some other source.

Suddenly, there was a vast explosion, and the car was engulfed in flames.

It was obvious that Schwarz would have very little chance. Hughes ran towards the flames with a fire extinguisher. His attempts were futile. Meanwhile Sharp telephoned hopelessly for an ambulance.

It was a minute or so before Sharp could look around for the old lady, although he knew she would be gone, probably in a box by now. He looked around the van, which was unlocked but empty. Then he went into the garden of the house outside which it was parked. There were a few long poles by the side of the path, but nothing else. He walked to the far end of the garden, where there was a hedge.

He parted the leaves, and saw a little white van vanishing into the distance along a farm track.

Now Will Sharp had a pretty fair idea what they were looking for.

All the airports, the Channel ports and the Eurotunnel were alerted.

Jacques Calmet was arrested as he tried to board a ferry in Dover.

There was all the evidence one needed in the back of his little white Renault van.

It was 1941. Maria Legrand was in her late teens, and living in Amiens. It seemed a particularly cold winter, and the accommodation in which her family was lodging had no heating. Not that they would be staying there long. They never stayed anywhere long. Her theatrical family moved almost continuously, not solely because of the need to perform all over Europe, but also because of their difficulty in paying bills.

Maria decided she wanted a more stable existence.

But that wasn't easy, as the theatre was in her blood, and she felt uneasy away from that world.

After much deliberation, she decided to capitalise on one of her talents.

She moved to Paris, gambled on taking a lease on a very small building she felt could be adapted as a puppet theatre, and opened it to the public a few weeks later.

Her gamble paid off, and very soon she had established not only one of the most reputable puppet theatres in France, but also a thriving school for puppeteers.

She also changed the name of her act to 'Maria Metz et ses Marionnettes.'

Jacques Calmet had been her most devoted and ardent pupil.

It was to his house in Lens that Maria had been invited after her eviction, but she had suffered a stroke during the voyage and had died in Jacques' arms soon after her arrival.

Jacques resolved to use his consummate puppetry skills to bring down the firm of 'Galsworthy, Dickens, and Schwarz.' That appealed to his sense of justice.

He had watched the partners' routines for some weeks before deciding on Galsworthy as his first victim.

He had carried one of his favourite marionettes, a little girl he called Cassandre, up to the balcony of the little bistro above a small lane opposite Galsworthy's house (it was chilly, so he was the only one outside). There he waited whilst Galsworthy fussed over his rubbish bags, and waited for the first heavy vehicle.

As it drew level, he lowered Cassandre into the lane, pulled her strings, and the little puppet wandered quickly into the road. He would have been heart-broken if any harm had come to her, but the driver was thankfully alert, and swerved to avoid her. Afterwards he pulled her back up to the balcony, and disappeared with her as quickly as he could.

It *had* been a coincidence that the tanker had belonged to a company in which Galsworthy and his partners had a controlling interest, but it wasn't really too surprising. The finance company had an interest in just about every local firm, and the dairy was no exception. Its tankers were up and down that road almost continuously, or so it seemed to the residents.

Calmet changed his plans in the light of this coincidence, for he knew of most of Galsworthy, Dickens, and Schwarz's investments.

He needed his puppetry skills even more for his next murder.

This time, he actually used Dickens' body, suitable concussed, as the puppet.

Using a system of pulleys and ropes, he controlled Dickens from the tree branch over the road. He concealed the body initially behind the trunk, and then juggled the ropes to give the impression that Dickens was leaving the concealment of the trunk, jumping over the ditch, and into the path of the tanker.

After the first murder, he knew that Milk! tankers did not have phones installed. While George Mills went to old Cain's house to phone for the ambulance, Calmet removed the ropes and other impedimenta, and then went back to his van (when he was spotted by Mills carrying what he thought was fishing equipment).

Having now successfully focussed everyone's attention on Milk! he made the Sunday morning phone call to Schwarz, knowing there was only one route he could take. Having previously removed the petrol tank cover on his car, and having liberally sprayed petrol over where he knew he would crash, he was all set.

Hiding behind the blue van (stolen, of course) he used a long pole to swing the old lady puppet into the path of the car, closely followed by the pram.

"The rest you know," Sharp concluded. "All the puppets were in the back of the van, but Jacques Calmet was quite happy to confess, anyway."

"He said he'd done everything he needed to do."

Interval

The evening was now becoming more convivial and less formal than it had previously been. The stories were becoming more frequently interrupted by members of the audience moving up to the table to recharge their glasses or reload their plates.

As if it had been waiting for the last story to end, a bat flew in through an open window, circled the room briefly, and then left again.

The cat also left, having shared its passengers freely.

Thomas John was next.

The Little Lady Vanishes

The Desk Sergeant wasn't too perturbed to hear that Miss Alice Ash had "just vanished into thin air," as in his experience it seemed to happen to young girls all the time these days.

However, he couldn't be too blunt with her parents, as they were plainly distressed, and so he took far more notes than he would normally have done under the circumstances, and said that he was sure that she was all right, and that she'd be home in the morning, and that there was no need for them to worry.

But Mr. and Mrs. Ash did worry, and didn't sleep all night.

Nevertheless, they waited until 8.00 a.m. before telephoning the Police Station at Wayzcroft again. Which was unfortunate, as it didn't open on Saturdays (or Sundays or Mondays for that matter).

They knew someone at Mayne Police Station and so got through to him. He was more sympathetic, and a Sergeant called around within the hour.

"Alice is normally such a good girl, maybe not really religious, but very very moral," they sobbed in chorus. "Something dreadful must have happened to her."

"Now, now, there" said Sergeant Withey, realising he was sounding uncannily like Mr. Plod in the Noddy television series. "What actually happened?"

Mr. Ash, Gordon, began first.

"Well, Alice went to that terrible disco in Mayne on Friday night. The Christian Fellowship Dance I think it's called. She always caught the last bus home, Wayz Bus Services, leaving Mayne at 2223, that's twenty-three minutes past ten o'clock, isn't it?"

"Yes, yes," Mrs. Ash continued impatiently, "And the bus driver, that nice man with the big nose, said she had definitely got on the bus there at 10.23. It stops right outside our house, so we were waiting for it at 10.35, but there wasn't anybody on board, well, not our Alice anyway. The driver said she couldn't have got off anywhere without his knowing. She'd just vanished into thin air."

"Of course, we've checked with all her friends. She doesn't tend to have many, but she's very close to the ones she does have. Her best friend is Delia Carr, who lives near Acorn Cross, but she didn't stay there. We've checked everyone else we can think of, and she didn't stay the night with any of them."

"Are there any close relatives?"

"She hasn't many in the area," Gordon Ash continued, "But she has begun to get rather friendly recently with her Aunt Sybil. She and her Uncle George live not far from Delia."

"I'd better have a recent photograph," Withey asked. He was spoilt for choice.

Bert Worsley was enjoying a day off from driving, as he had worked up to his legal limit. He was mowing the lawn when Withey called at his house, having got his address from Wayz Bus Services.

"Yes, it's funny that. I know Mr. and Mrs. Ash. I mean, they usually wait outside the house for, er, Alison, is it? Alice, yes."

"Alice definitely got on the bus at Mayne. I'd know her without having to look at all those photographs. She got on, showed her return ticket, and then sat right at the back in the middle. That's at the far end of the aisle, so I could hardly miss her whenever I looked in the mirror. Not that I needed to look into it that often, as we only use it to check on the passengers. We use the outside mirrors for looking at the traffic behind. But the crowd that night were all people I knew. They were all O.K., as was Alice, unlike some of the late-night passengers we get."

"Anyway, the journey was pretty uneventful. We left Mayne on time (well, I wasn't going to hang around for the really late-night revellers), and there's a fast drive along the inner by-pass as far as the request stop at Acorn Cross. I did check once or twice, and Alice was certainly at the back all that time. There was nobody waiting at Acorn Cross, and no-one asked to get off, so I didn't stop there, but I must have waited a minute or so at the junction with the Great Wayz Road. There was a lot of traffic, and I reckon they should install lights. I didn't let anyone off the bus there, though."

"Then there was another fast run to the stop outside Alice's house. She wasn't on the bus by then though. We searched everywhere, not that there are many hiding places on a modern bus. The other passengers were four elderly couples who had been playing bingo in Mayne. They helped, but, as I said, there's not much space to hide."

Sergeant Withey interrupted him, "Surely there was some way she could have got off the bus somewhere?"

"Well, she certainly didn't get off through the front door. There are only three other exits. There's an inspection hatch in the floor, but here's hardly space to drop through there, and you need a special carriage key - it's T-shaped - to open it. Anyway, it's in the aisle, so I could hardly have missed someone opening that."

"The other exits are emergency exits, one on each side of the coach: a door on the offside, and a window on the nearside. But they're both fitted with micro-switches. If anyone opens one of these emergency exits, an alarm goes off."

"And we have to have these switches fitted and functioning properly under British law. They're pretty unreliable, mind you, but, if they don't work, the Ministry has the power to stop us using the coach until it's fixed."

"Anyway, if she'd used one of these exits, the alarm would have sounded. There's even a sticker - they're quite big - warning "Beware this door is alarmed." She would have seen those clearly enough, even at night, as I had all the interior lights on."

"Can I see the coach?" asked Withey.

"Oh, it'll be in the yard in Wayzcroft. It's in for a service today."

Indeed, the coach was easily found, standing in the middle of the yard. The yard itself had not been so easily found: Withey had eventually tracked it down right in the middle of Wayzcroft town, at the far end of a long narrow cul-de-sac of terraced houses off the main street.

He sought the yard foreman, or whatever he styled himself.

"That'll be the one." He checked the registration number that Withey had written in his notepad, which he had flipped open in what he hoped was a suitably impressive style.

"It's a K-reg. Ford Plaxton 53-seater that we bought new six years ago, with a grant from the council," he said. "Bert usually drives it on the late afternoon and evening runs to Mayne. Climb aboard if you like. It's just been serviced, but it's probably not been cleaned yet."

The coach was, in fact, decidedly grubby. Several seats had torn moquette, most of them inexpertly patched. But there were no other exits other than the front double doors, the floor hatch, and the two emergency exits.

Withey opened each emergency exit several times. A quite strident alarm sounded each time. And each door was clearly marked as having such an alarm.

Willie Withey sat down on the back seat of the coach to think, suddenly realising that he was seated almost exactly where young Alice Ash had sat on her fateful journey. The foreman had since departed, obviously feeling that a member of the Police force could be trusted. Withey found a ten-pence coin on the floor and pocketed it.

Alice had clearly got onto the coach, and equally clearly had not been there on its arrival at Wayzcroft. Some of his colleagues had already checked with the other passengers on the coach, and they had confirmed that the girl had not returned past them along the aisle during the journey. So, she must have got out through the back door. If she had done it quickly, perhaps when the coach had started off at the Great Wayz Road, would the driver had felt the door opening and shutting? But what about the alarm? Could she have started to open the door, inserted something, a piece of plastic perhaps, and stopped the alarm from sounding? Withey tried to do it. He couldn't. The alarm rang out loudly each time.

Would the driver have heard the alarm, if *another* noise had sounded at the same time? But how could Alice have known another noise would happen simultaneously, to cover the noise of the alarm? Alternatively, could she have created such a noise?

He gave up and phoned the Station. Other members of the force had by now visited the girl's friends, most of whom lived near Acorn Cross, but no one had heard from the girl since Friday.

He decided to visit the parents again, to see if there were any news.

There wasn't, so he checked the address of Uncle George and Aunt Sybil and called on them. He began to feel that Acorn Cross was where everything and everyone of any importance to this disappearance seemed to be associated.

Aunt Sybil, Mrs. Wordsworth, answered the door. She was short and rotund, and appeared to be constantly beleaguered by her several offspring (waiting for them to stand still sufficiently long enough to allow a head count seemed impossible).

"Alice? Lovely girl. We didn't used to see much of her, except at Christmas, of course, but she's been calling around every week or so of late. Nothing's happened to her, has it?"

"We hope not," Withey replied, feeling rather less than confident. "Is your husband here?"

"No, I'm afraid not. He's away in Malaga at some sort of conference. Double- and triple-glazing, that sort of thing. He's an executive with Wayz Windows. You can get in touch through his office if you want to contact him, I suppose."

Wayz Windows' head office confirmed that he was indeed at the Clearly Better Group Symposium, rather to Withey's surprise. They gave him all the details of the flight and the hotel.

He contacted the local airport who confirmed that he had flown out on a fairly early (but naturally much later than scheduled) flight on the Saturday morning.

The reservation was for Mr. Wordsworth and his wife.

Back at the Station, Withey tried to think it out.

He was now convinced that Alice had slipped off the coach whilst it waited at the Great Wayz Road junction, intent on a late-night rendezvous with her Uncle, before flying off to Spain.

But how had she got off the coach undetected, without the buzzer sounding?

Suddenly, he had a thought. The alarm buzzer on the emergency exit of the coach was working satisfactorily now, but what if that were only because it had been repaired during the routine service, to comply with legal requirements?

Young Alice could have slipped through the door whilst the coach was at the Great Wayz Road, walked the few yards to Chez Wordsworth, and then caught the flight a few hours later.

He phoned the coach depot. After what seemed hours of waiting, the foreman answered the phone. The mechanics had all gone home he said, but the service sheets were kept on clipboards hanging from a notice board, and so he went to check them.

Another eternity later, the foreman confirmed that the emergency door buzzer had been found "dysfunctional" and fixed.

Sergeant Withey stood up and cheered triumphantly.

Withey's superiors agreed it should be sorted out at once, or as soon as practicable, bearing in mind that the couple were on foreign soil, and that it was now late on Sunday. They managed to find a Spanish translator and arranged for him to be in attendance at the Station in Mayne first thing on Monday morning. Then Withey or one of his superiors would ask him to contact their opposite numbers in Spain (the D.C.I. had met some members of a Spanish police force at some conference or other, and felt sure they were from Malaga). It was decided that nothing "too flashy" was required, but that perhaps someone from the Spanish force could pop over to the Hotel and verify the facts.

On Monday morning, one of the Wayz Bus Services' single-deckers was involved in an accident on the Great Wayz Road. The driver, clearly not as cautious as Bert Worsley, had tried to edge out into the traffic, but had remained stuck halfway across the junction for quite a while, relying on others to note the situation and stop.

Most of them did. However, a local farmer driving an old Volvo had not noticed the bus as he sought in vain for Radio 4.

The resulting congestion blocked the whole of the junction, across which Sergeant Withey needed to cross. He was stuck in the jam for twenty minutes.

Whilst waiting, he went over the case in his mind.

If Alice had slipped out of back of the coach, she was lucky that the alarm was not working. What he still couldn't understand was why she had risked it, when the alarm was clearly marked (and he had managed to read the sign easily even in a fairly dim light).

If she wanted to go off for a holiday with her lover, why hadn't she just taken a taxi from Mayne, or asked him to collect her from the disco by car?

Perhaps she had *wanted* to be noticed? Perhaps her apparently high moral attitude had made her ashamed of her affair. If she had felt powerless to stop it, was she hoping someone would find out and intervene. Was it a cry for help?

Withey suddenly realised *exactly* what must have happened.

"Oh no," he shouted, to nobody in particular.

He sounded his horn to a colleague he recognised, who was trying to disentangle the congestion. As the traffic had now started to ease, he was able to wave him through ahead of the rest of the traffic.

He could have stopped and telephoned, but decided that it would be better to drive as fast as he could to the Station.

When he arrived there, his superior, Lucas, and a local schoolteacher who called himself Senor Watkins were relaxing in the most luxurious office in the Station.

"We've already arranged it, all on our own," Lucas said, beaming.

"I got straight through to Mr. Lucas's friend, who was *just* the person to contact," Senor Watkins smirked. "I explained most carefully what was the problem, and they said they'd get onto it straight away."

Senor Watkins smirked again, in case Withey had missed it first time.

"I think you'd better get back to them, and ask them to wait for a little while," Withey said.

Senor Watkins looked to Lucas for assurance.

Sergeant Withey explained what his thinking. Lucas' face drained of colour, and he told Watkins to get back on the telephone and stop them.

Senor Watkins put the phone down.

"We were a little late I'm afraid. I think your friends in Spain must have looked upon it as a chance to prove themselves to their English counterparts and perhaps get some publicity."

Lucas closed his eyes and groaned.

"I think they misinterpreted me. I just don't know *how* they could have done. But it appears a small group of them more or less stormed the hotel, and forced their way into Senor Wordsworth's room, only to find him in bed with someone who was not really his wife. But she was a thirty-eight year old Indian lady from Macclesfield. Not really Alice at all."

Lucas opened his eyes," Did you ask them to keep the press out of this?"

Senor Watkins made a final comment, "It seems they had expressly invited the newspapers along to record their example of international police cooperation." He excused himself and headed for the toilets.

Lucas turned to Withey, "Do you know where Alice really is?"

Withey nodded. "I think I do," he said.

"This morning, waiting in the traffic jam, I realised that, although she had managed to slip off the bus undetected, she probably hadn't expected to, because there were notices plastered all over the windows warning of the alarm."

"She had clearly *wanted* to make a grand exit, as it were, to leave a trail, and to make it perfectly clear where people would assume she had gone."

"I can imagine her standing in the road in the cold night air, the open coach door in her hands, and no sound whatsoever. That must have been quite a shock to her. Then the coach drove off, and the door quietly shut."

"She had clearly become very friendly with her Aunt Sybil, and must have found out about George Wordsworth's affair. I think it must have been a fairly obvious and unsubtle liaison. As she had a high moral sense, she wanted to expose him and let his wife know all about it, or bring her to her senses, or whatever."

"She wanted to make it look as if it were *she* spending the holiday in Spain with her Uncle. She knew her parents would get the Police involved, and so generate as much publicity as possible to expose George Wordsworth. Actually, she must have spent the night at a friend's, probably at her best friend's house nearby." With a flourish, Withey indicated the house they were approaching.

Prior to this visit, they had telephoned Mrs. Wordsworth to explain and apologise and do whatever they hoped was necessary.

Now, they could see Mrs. Wordsworth standing outside the house they were approaching. She was arguing and screaming at a short, pasty-faced young girl.

"Look here, Alice, don't you think I knew all about George? I've put up with his dirty little affairs for years! I hate him as much as you do, but he brings in the money, and I love the kids. Thanks to your stupid interfering, what the hell am I going to do now?" She switched from anger to tears in seconds, and collapsed onto a seat in the porch.

Lucas and Withey decided to interview Alice at a later time.

Interval

It was now getting late, although perhaps not so late by students' standards (and lecturers have long been expected to conform to these youthful hours). Mrs. Guiteras had some time previously tendered her apologies and retired to bed.

"Mmm," the Professor said, looking around the room thoughtfully, as might some hungry owl in a room full of plump mice.

"Dorothy L. Sayers next, I think," he pronounced.

Miss Hermione P. Sayers arose, apparently perfectly happy with her nickname. She had been given it because she was often to be found engrossed in one of the Lord Peter Wimsey stories. Her claim of being distantly related was treated with a considerable degree of suspicion, however.

Downwardly Mobile

Darren Hopkins was that sort of person who has to acquire every new gadget as soon as it appears on the market (or, in the case of most of his purchases, even before it officially reaches our shores). He was the first in his street to buy a mobile phone, and felt it such an indispensable part of his lifestyle that he was rarely seen without one. Not that his latest phone, flown over from some Asian country especially for him, could be easily seen: it had more features than any of his previous nineteen phones, but was so small it could fit inside his ticket pocket. It could only actually be seen when he used it, which was alas all too often.

His girlfriend of many years, Shirley Jones, had agreed to accompany him on a short walk along Brightstone Beach one February morning. She had been only too happy to comply with Darren's request to sit in a secluded corner under the cliff-face, but would have been less happy had she known that he only wanted to test the sensitivity of his new phone. However, she never discovered this as their conversation was interrupted by the arrival of John Christopher ... very fast ... and in a downward direction.

John Christopher had fallen from the cliff almost immediately above them.

Darren therefore had rather more justification than usual to try out his new phone, and called for help straight away.

Not that help was of any use to John Christopher. The cliff was sixty feet high at that point.

Inspector Burke also had a mobile phone, if more than twice the size of Darren Hopkins' phone. As he was coincidentally at the nearby Coastguard Station with some constables at the time of John Christopher's demise, he and his team were able to walk along the beach and reach the cliff-face within a few minutes.

John Christopher was dressed in casual but warm outdoor clothing that gave the impression of being quite expensive, but which was probably very expensive. Inspector Burke thought that he looked like a fairly senior accountant, probably retired ... although, under the circumstances he thought, definitely retired. His hair was grey in a rather distinguished way, and was certainly well-groomed. His nails were also well-manicured, but, surprisingly, there were slight traces of some oil, perhaps engine oil, on his fingers. There was very little in his pockets: a wallet with more credit cards than actual money, a personal organiser, a set of car keys, and a large hotel key on an oversized key ring to deter residents from taking keys out of the hotel. He put these into one of the plastic bags he always kept in his pocket.

Inspector Burke was on the point of calling for a medical expert and an ambulance when there was a scream from behind him.

"Oh God, it's John." A tall, well-dressed woman, still extremely attractive for her fifty-five years or so, had approached the small group without being noticed. She seemed highly agitated, but unwilling to move any closer.

"I'm afraid he's dead, " Inspector Burke said quietly, unable to think of any better way of putting it at that moment. "He fell from the cliff above, and ..." He waved his left arm vaguely.

The woman, after a while, calmed down a little. "That's my husband, John Christopher. I'm Christina Christopher. We live in Birmingham, but we're on a walking holiday here, and we're staying at the 'Little Rock Hotel' in the next bay. It's the penultimate day of the holiday, so I had hoped we could have taken a break from trudging all over the countryside, but my husband thought otherwise. I wanted to visit the shops in Exeter, but John said we could visit shops anytime, and insisted on doing his favourite walk again today. So, I took the car off to Exeter, and he walked along the cliff path." She looked up and winced a little.

"Anyway, after I'd driven a few miles, I thought that I didn't really want to be away from him. Our marriage has had its ups and downs recently, and it seemed churlish to exacerbate any such problems. It was, after all, one of our few real chances to be together. My husband was an accountant, and he worked very long hours. So I turned the car around to come and join him, parked up on the top over there, and, when I saw all of you down on the beach, I thought, I hope that isn't ..."

Inspector Burke thought of the oil on John Christopher's fingers. "Are you having problems with your car?" he asked.

Mrs. Christopher looked a little surprised.

"No," she replied, "The car's running fine. Do you think I could be alone with my husband for a minute?"

This seemed an odd request from a woman who appeared not to be the sentimental sort, but it was the kind of request that was difficult to refuse. Out of the corner of his eye, Inspector Burke noted that she checked her husband's pockets.

After a few seconds, Mrs. Christopher announced that she felt that she ought to return to the hotel for "a lie-down." Despite her protestations, the Inspector insisted on accompanying her back to her car.

There was something wrong with all this, he felt.

The Saab was parked not far from where the Inspector had parked his car before visiting the Coastguard Station (this being a rather beautiful stretch of countryside, car parks were notoriously uncommon).

"Thank you very much, Inspector. I shall be all right now," Mrs. Christopher said.

"I'll just wait until you get the car started," the Inspector replied helpfully.

After a few minutes of Mrs. Christopher's obvious prevarication, Inspector Burke said, "You only have one set of keys to this car, don't you?" Mrs. Christopher nodded. "And I think I have them in my pocket, don't I, Mrs. Christopher?" Mrs. Christopher nodded again.

Inspector Burke relaxed a little, and leant against the Saab. "I don't know exactly what happened, but it was something like this, wasn't it?"

"You set off from the hotel in the car on your own this morning, in the direction of Exeter, after your husband had left for his walk. You probably made sure that enough people witnessed your departure. After a few miles, you turned back towards the coast, and met your husband on the road from the hotel. As an excuse for returning to join him on the walk, you complained of some problem with the car. He got in to test the car, and drove to the nearest car park, where he looked unsuccessfully under the bonnet for a while, trying to identify the non-existent problem. He was probably pleased when you announced that you had changed your mind about coming on the walk with him. It was only when you arrived back at the car park after having pushed him over the edge of the cliff that you realised he had kept the car keys after driving to the car park."

"If it hadn't been for Darren Hopkins' mobile phone, it would probably have taken so long for us to get out here that you could have retrieved the keys, and driven on to Exeter."

"Yes," Mrs. Christopher said, her eyes a little distant, "What *are* the shops like in Exeter?"

Interval

Mike Summers was the next to take the rostrum.

Get Off the Earth

"So, if my police force can't find a man with a fully-grown African elephant in an area with a very limited radius, the public is bound to feel that perhaps we're not competent to handle *any* sort of police work."

"And I don't suppose I'd blame them, either."

The Chief Constable let his hands fall into his lap, resignedly.

"It's a bit like Houdini's vanishing elephant illusion, isn't it?" said Simon Wing.

"Not really," replied the Chief Constable with more than a trace of irritation in his voice. "This wasn't done in front of an audience, and the elephant really has disappeared. Have you any useful ideas?"

He did not sound very hopeful.

Simon Wing came away from the window, from where he had been staring at his prized lupins, and stretched out on his favourite sofa. "Well, I have been watching the news with considerable interest, and I have one idea, but perhaps you'd fill in the details first for me. I'm sure the important but unsensational elements have been largely ignored by the press."

"Actually, they haven't missed much, if anything."

"Let's see. It all started, God, was it really only the day before yesterday?"

"Henry Masterson is the owner of Masterson's, one of the few long-established circuses to have been able to survive into recent times, although I'm not sure if they can last much longer now."

"Most circuses have a side of the business for which they're particularly famous, and, with Masterson's, it's elephants. That's what most people go to see their circus shows for, anyway."

"The day before yesterday, around four in the morning, some of the circus folk were awoken by the sound of Henry Masterson having an almighty row with his wife, Cordelia. They've been married for years, but things have been a little shaky of late … to say the least."

"We've had to piece things together from what the witnesses heard and what evidence there was."

"She must have stormed out of the house, or rather the caravan. That's not to say that it's one of these insubstantial little things cars tow. Circus folk mostly seem to live in huge, comfortable trailers, and, being the ringmaster and owner, Henry's home really is like a house on wheels. It was parked alongside where the elephants are kept. All the elephants are under Henry's personal supervision, and apparently no-one else goes near them. Since his disappearance, they've had to bring his father out of retirement to look after them."

"So, Henry tries to settle down in the trailer, but he hears a noise coming from the elephant enclosure, and so he goes to investigate. To his horror, his wife is taking her anger out on his beloved elephants. He lashes out at his wife, she falls, bangs her head, and … well, I don't think it would ever have been considered as murder, but …"

"Anyway, Henry must have thought otherwise, and he decides to make a run for it … but not without taking one of his elephants with him."

"So, he makes his escape … God, this sounds stupid … along with a fully-grown African elephant. It was apparently his favourite, and it may have been the one that Cordelia was attacking, so he may have taken it to try and help it recover from its ordeal. It may have been a decision of the moment: if he were planning on marching with it across the surrounding farmland, he would have wanted to be off before everyone was up and about."

"This is what the enclosure looked like when we got to it."

The Chief Constable leant over and handed Simon a series of photographs of the elephant enclosure. On one side was a line of ten elephant pens, the largest on the left, each adjoining pen being slightly smaller in size. The gate of the largest pen was open. "That's Rajah's pen" the Chief Constable pointed out. All the other pens to the right were each occupied by an elephant of gradually-decreasing size until the final few at the end each contained a younger, smaller elephant. Simon thought that, considering that Henry Masterson was renowned for the way he looked after his elephants, some of them looked a little short of space in their pens.

Cordelia's body lay in a small patch of blood near the rightmost cage.

"We've examined the site thoroughly. There is nowhere anyone could hide an elephant, and we've checked and re-checked the numbers: there's definitely one missing."

"We investigated how they might have made their escape, but all the large circus vehicles hadn't been moved. The only vehicle unaccounted for is a small Ford Transit van, which is certainly not big enough for a large elephant. It's got the name of the circus emblazoned on its sides and it's brightly-coloured.. But, as it's the smallest vehicle there, it's often borrowed for various personal uses by the circus folk, so it may have nothing to do with the case at all. I can't see how it can anyway, because it's just not big enough."

"And there haven't been any reports of large vehicles being stolen or hired in the area."

"So, they must have just walked off, but we can't find any witnesses to or evidence of their escape, nor of any place where they might be hiding within a considerable radius … and there are very few places where you can hide an elephant around here."

"So, what's your theory, Simon?" the Chief Constable said more hopefully.

Simon Wing clicked his tongue a few times.

"Right. So your problem is simply that someone has walked off with a fully-grown African elephant, which nobody has seen since, which is no longer on the site, and which isn't hidden anywhere in the immediate vicinity … and the only means of transportation is a small Transit van?"

"Well, in that case there's only one solution, eh?"

"Henry Masterson is a showman, so it seems natural that he would have used a showman's trick."

"An old magician's trick is to make an animal or a bird in a cage vanish, to the amazement of the audience. What the audience doesn't realise is that the small creature is actually very cheap to buy, and the magician has crushed it under a heavy false bottom within the cage."

"It would take a hell of a big weight to crush an elephant," muttered the Chief Constable.

Simon continued, "Maybe, but what if he takes the elephant and disposes of it soon after he leaves the circus site? He'd need somewhere like an abandoned mine shaft, a cave, or something like that. There'd be no traces of the elephant, and he could escape in the small van and travel as far as he liked, far outside your radius of enquiry, probably abroad."

"How does that sound, then?"

The Chief Constable looked unimpressed. "We're not as daft as the press make out, you know. We've thought of that. Not only have we searched everywhere where a living elephant might be hidden, we've also searched for anywhere where an elephant could have been killed and dumped."

Simon Wing looked crestfallen. "So that's not the solution, then?"

"I'm afraid not."

It was after numerous cups of coffee, taken as a stimulant, but singularly ineffective, that the Chief Constable realised he was getting nowhere and decided to leave. He declined an offer of staying for tea having seen the state of Simon's kitchen.

He said farewell, and left Simon standing at his front door. "Maybe they just vanished off the face of the earth, eh?" he added as a final throw-away line. After a curve in the path, just out of sight of the house, he hacked desultorily at a few lupins.

Simon thought for a few seconds and then clicked his tongue. He ran down the path and just managed to stop the Chief Constable as he was driving away.

The Chief Constable looked even more irritated than he had at any time that afternoon.

"Look, I'm not sure," stuttered Simon, "But I think I may have an idea."

Back in his front parlour, Simon began to explain.

"I was right that it was a showman's trick, but I had the wrong showman and the wrong trick."

"Have you ever heard of Sam Loyd? Have you ever heard of his 'Get Off the Earth' puzzle?"

The Chief Constable shook his head, still visibly irritated.

"Well, he designed a puzzle which consists of a circular drawing of the world, which can be rotated in the middle of a larger card."

"And ... ?" muttered the Chief Constable.

"Around the edge of the rotating world are drawn thirteen Chinese warriors, most of them drawn partly on the earth, and partly on the surrounding card. The proportion of each figure on and off the earth varies progressively around its circumference: the first is wholly on the earth, the last is entirely on the surrounding card."

"But, when you turn the earth so that each Chinese warrior lines up with the next, there are only twelve to be seen. So where has this thirteenth figure vanished?"

"I have no idea," said the Chief Constable, suppressing "And I don't much care" under his breath.

"Well, basically, when the world is rotated, each split figure breaks up into two parts, and the part on the earth is then combined with what is a slightly larger part off the earth. So, instead of thirteen warriors, we have twelve figures, each thirteen-twelfths of the original size."

"This isn't getting us anywhere, is it, Mr. Wing?" spluttered the Chief Constable. "Are you seriously suggesting that Henry Masterson replaced the ten original elephants in the pens with nine elephants each …" he screwed up his eyes in concentration, and started moving his fingers, "… ten-ninths of their original size?"

"No, no. What he did was merely to move each elephant into the adjoining smaller pen."

The Chief Constable now had a slightly glazed expression in his eyes.

"That's why each elephant seemed a little too large for its pen."

"However, I suppose the analogy isn't perfect, as the missing elephant didn't disappear, but was removed."

Simon continued, "Rajah, the elephant you and your force have been searching for, is still there, but not in his pen. He's in the adjoining pen."

"The elephant you should have been looking for is the smallest. That's probably the one most likely to have been targeted by Henry's wife anyway, as it would be the most vulnerable. And Cordelia's body was found lying next to the smallest cage."

"The smallest elephant could just have fitted into the Transit van, allowing Henry to drive off anywhere he liked, although he probably wouldn't have dared try and drive abroad with an elephant in the back."

"So you can widen your search throughout the whole of Great Britain now. The van must be pretty eye-catching, so you shouldn't have too much trouble finding witnesses and tracing the vehicle."

The Chief Constable left Simon's house in a much happier frame of mind this time. He was still a little puzzled as to where the thirteen Chinese warriors fitted into the case, though.

"Or was it twelve?" he said aloud.

Interval

There was a slight commotion at this stage, as somebody started complaining about animal cruelty in circuses, and somebody else said that it was "only a story, so shut up."

Professor Guiteras tried to calm them down, it has to be said fairly unsuccessfully, and so decided to hurry on with the next story.

Professor Guiteras turned to Pamela Lewis and asked, "Is your story about animal cruelty, dear?"

On receiving a negative reply, he requested her story.

A Load of Old Rubbish

Joshua Henton had always been inordinately proud of his matchstick model of the 'Titanic.' It was actually based on a photograph of some other ship he had seen in a magazine somewhere, but he had added a fourth funnel to it, and felt that this conferred some degree of authenticity upon it. It wasn't even a particularly good model: whether because of a lack of confidence in his ability, or because he was a non-smoker with limited resources, he had decided to construct it to such a scale that the finished model was only eight inches long. The fact that it was made of matchsticks was therefore painfully obvious, and many of the ship's features were much distorted by the relatively large size of the materials used.

Nevertheless, old Joshua had decided that the model should take up the most prominent place in his lounge, and so had put it in the centre of the large table there. He had always looked after it and had lavished as much care upon it as he possibly could during his lifetime, and, even as his bloodied head lay against it in death, he seemed to have arranged himself to rest against it as gently as possible.

An ornamental poker with only a small smear of blood on it lay nearby.

"It doesn't really look like a burglary that went wrong, Sir," P.C. Bent said to break the silence, after his superior had been staring at the sight motionless for a while.

"Not really, but you never really know with the sort of amateurs we have to put up with these days," D.C.I. Deeks replied. "Who found the body?"

"One of his relatives. Normally he wouldn't have been found until the cleaning lady arrived around twelve o'clock. But a relative found the body just after eight this morning. His name is Walton Carey, and he lives just up this road. In fact, I think most of the relatives live in this road. Anyway, he was driving to work this morning around eight, when someone ran over a dog ..."

"What the hell has *that* got to do with all this?" snapped D.C.I. Deeks.

"Well, the road was blocked while someone tried to calm down the driver, so Mr. Carey had to stop outside for a few minutes, and that's when he noticed that the hall window was smashed. He parked his car and went to check, and that's when he found the body."

"What does the medical officer say?"

"Not a lot at the moment. Joshua Henton was killed by a single blow from the poker, around eleven last night. If you want more, you'll have to wait until he's completed his full and detailed report, but I got the impression that there won't be a great deal more."

"Was anything taken?"

"We haven't got a full list. We probably never will. There were lots of drawers open, and a few small china things smashed, but Mr. Carey could only confirm that a few pieces of silver, some very small antiques that *might* be worth something, and probably his wallet and a tin moneybox were missing. It still looks to me more like a murder that someone tried to disguise as a burglary."

"So you said. And you may be right, Son," D.C.I. Deeks said condescendingly. "Presumably the only ones to gain from a murder would be the relatives. They all live nearby, do they?"

"Yes, Mr. Carey lives at the other end of the road, and there are three other related families between there and this end of the road. It's only a small village, and it's just about the only road."

"When was our Mr. Henton last seen?"

"A neighbour saw him putting out his dustbin bag around eight last night. Being an elderly person - he was seventy-four - he probably wanted to retire early, but he was taking an awful risk of having his bag savaged by one of the neighbourhood dogs. I know: I live nearby."

"Mmm. I've seen enough. It's beginning to smell in here. Tell the boys they can clear up. I need some air."

In fact, D.C.I. Deeks was not so much motivated by a wish for clearer air, as by a need to pollute some himself. Once in the garden, he lit up a fag (he rolled his own rather inexpertly, and one could hardly describe them as cigarettes). He thought to himself for a while.

"Let's talk hypothetically, Son," he finally said. "What would you do if you burgled a house?"

"That depends on the sort of goods I'd stolen. If I'd got radios or video recorders or something like that, I'd probably try to flog them down the local pub. If I'd stolen antiques or gold or stones, then I'd have to find a fence, someone professional."

"O.K. What if you accidentally murdered someone during the burglary?"

"In that case, unless the haul were particularly lucrative, I'd probably try and find somewhere to dump the stuff as quickly as possible on my way back."

"You wouldn't want to have anything incriminating on you, would you?"

"It probably wouldn't be worth it if a murder were involved. In fact, I'd probably just leave the stuff in the house," P.C. Bent said.

"So, what would you do if you tried to cover up a murder with a burglary? In that case, you wouldn't even want the things you'd stolen ... *and* you probably wouldn't have any channels set up to dispose of the goods. But you'd have to take something to give the impression that a burglary had taken place. And you certainly wouldn't want the stuff in your own house ... and that could be a particular problem if you lived in the same road and didn't want to draw attention to yourself by travelling around unnecessarily in the middle of the night, dumping stolen property."

P.C. Bent nodded, "But, if you didn't expect the body to be found until lunch-time ..."

D.C.I. Deeks had started speaking, and had got as far as "At what time does the ... ?" when a large refuse disposal vehicle turned the corner. It sounded extremely asthmatic, and was painted in what the local council clearly thought was a shade of green that suggested its being environmentally-friendly. However, the amount of dirt and filth clinging to its exterior quickly dispelled any thoughts of its taking anything but an extremely hostile attitude towards its environment.

For such a clearly unfit person, D.C.I. Deeks moved remarkably quickly down the steps to the lumbering vehicle. P.C. Bent saw him converse with the driver, who initially shook his head vehemently. However, after D.C.I. Deeks had shown him his identification, and the driver had phoned someone in his organisation with more authority than he had, he seemed to become more enthusiastic. After a few minutes of conversation, he reversed his machine rather inexpertly back onto the main road, his face wreathed in smiles.

"Right, Son, all we need now is for me to phone the Station, and ask that nice W.P.C. Berry to knock up a little note on her computer to the effect that the rubbish will now be collected at seven this evening. Can you phone her, and arrange to have the notes delivered to all the houses in this street?"

P.C. Bent nodded, "So you managed to get the driver to agree to come back again this evening to collect the bags?"

"Er, no. Whether or not my little ploy works, I suppose *you*'ll have to collect them all, otherwise we'll get into a lot of trouble with the local Health Department."

Later, D.C.I. Deeks and P.C. Bent were parked as inconspicuously as possible in an unmarked police car towards one end of the road. By craning his neck, D.C.I. Deeks could see old Joshua Henton's house to the rear of the car. Ahead, more conveniently, they could see Walton Carey's house, and three other houses that they now had identified as belonging to the same family.

The notes that W.P.C. Berry had printed from her computer were just being delivered by a police constable who had taken his instructions to wear plain clothes to a rather scruffy extreme.

It wasn't too long a wait. The male head of the Henton-Carey household at number 15 emerged after a short while.

He looked around furtively, then picked up his black dustbin bag, and began to carry it up the steps into the house.

Turning, he was surprised to find D.C.I. Deeks and P.C. Bent following him up the steps as he carried the bag indoors.

Inside the bag, amongst the usual household detritus, were a few pieces of silver, some very small antiques that *might* be worth something, a wallet and a tin moneybox.

Interval

The impact of the denouement of the preceding story was somewhat diminished by a further disagreement about animal cruelty at the back of the room, as recriminations were thrown back and forth, and a half-full glass of a rather poor red Bordeaux (the Professor had kept the better wines for the beginning of the evening) had been tipped or thrown over someone.

After a considerable mopping-up exercise had been undertaken, and the situation soothed by a rather obviously-expensive bottle of wine being exhumed, Professor Guiteras called upon Nerd McQueeg.

Nerd McQueeg was obviously not his real name, and was not the one he wrote on his examination papers, but he liked the name, and people felt it suited him, and so it had stuck.

What the background of either the name or the person was nobody really knew ... or wanted to know, as he stood out as the closest in that academic year to a genuine eccentric, and was much valued as such.

Going for Baroque

"POLICE TRACE MURDERER AFTER DNA TESTING 36,000"

"SADISTIC SLAYER SHOPPED BY SHOCKED SPOUSE"

"VICIOUS KILLER CONFESSES TO POLICE"

It seems all too often that we see headlines like these in our local papers. It makes you think that perhaps our Police force has lost any ability to solve crimes except by a brainless tramping from door to door asking questions, or by relying on friends and acquaintances of the felon to do the Law's job for it, or even by boring the perpetrator of the crime so much and for so long that he gives himself up through sheer monotony.

If the Police ever had any ability, that is.

Why cannot the Police show the same inventive and logical deductive abilities we read about in detective stories?

Or perhaps the problem lies with us, the law-abiding and not so law-abiding members of the public.

Why don't people in real-life commit murders like those in Agatha Christie novels?

Napoleons of Crime, or even felons with some slight degree of ingenuity, don't seem to exist outside the realms of detective fiction.

Are we all so unimaginative that we can't create a masterwork of crime?

It seems to fall to me to correct this sorry state of affairs.

If I were to commit a murder, it would be a stroke of genius, a masterpiece of invention, my magnum opus!

And I shall.

Perhaps, I should introduce myself.

My name is Simon Boyle.

I suppose my most impressive feature is my intelligence: I have an I.Q. of over 160. I have to say that I usually find education so easy that it becomes a bore. In both Junior and High School, I was always top of the class in every subject (apart from sport, of course), and that without the slightest effort at all. All the time that I should have spent reading and revising I spent indulging myself in my interests, probably the most important of which was baroque music. I think I can say that my fame as a virtuoso of the harpsichord has spread far and wide across the musical globe.

Oxford came as a slight shock, I suppose. Suddenly, I found myself amongst the top intellectuals in the country.

Of course, I was able to cope, or at least I *could* have coped by myself.

But, honestly, the thought of actually having to work and read and all that sort of thing, just as the other poor fools have to do, really rather disgusted me.

Luckily, I was able to change rooms, and move in with Ronald Hancock, who was taking the same courses as I was. Not only was he perfectly happy to help me out with my theses and other work, but he was also intelligent, rather beautiful, and homosexual. We got on very well indeed.

It was only towards the beginning of my third year that I met Crispin Edwards-Carter.

Crispin was as handsome as Ronald, but had something that I realised I would soon be needing, something that Ronald could never give me … wealth! Crispin was very, very rich, his family having a large estate in Surrey, although, to be fair, not the best part of Surrey. He was also overtly well-bred (although, of course, not ostentatiously so), and we were in love.

But what was I to do with loyal Ronald?

I decided that, in order to remove Ronald from my life completely, I would also have to remove him from his.

Ronald was unfortunately involved with drugs, in a mild way one has to admit. Thus, I reasoned, it should be easy to get him into some drug-induced slumber, and then, well, hit him over the head, or something like that.

But the main problem was that I should be the chief, and probably only, suspect, so I needed an alibi.

I had to devise some scenario in which Ronald would be killed whilst I could conclusively prove that I could not have done it, and thus be above suspicion. I went over and over various plans and ideas, considering every suitable method of killing him and what would happen afterwards, rather as one would play chess (which I consider an abhorrent game, solely played by the masses to suggest they have some slight degree of misused intelligence). Indeed, I became quite obsessed with the idea of getting Ronald out of the way, to the extent that it seemed to take over every aspect of my life. But finally I felt I had the perfect plan. What I had worked out was, I was sure, foolproof.

I decided to go ahead as soon as possible.

Friday evening dawned, if that isn't a contradiction.

What better alibi, I reasoned, than for me to be performing in a baroque concert at the very time of poor Ronald's demise?

There was a small hall a few doors down from our room. I had played there a few times and so knew the layout there quite well. The hall dated from the 1920's (as did my draughty rooms) and had been built, not only for musical concerts, but also for amateur dramatics. What suited my purposes was that there was a small trap door set into the floor of the stage, and a fairly sound upright piano available. I had negotiated to hire the hall from 7.30 p.m. to 9.30 p.m. that Friday evening, and had asked my good friend, Adrian Sidoli, to share the limelight with me with his rather unexceptional guitar-playing. We had played together before, and had similar tastes in music, if not the same degree of accomplishment. If I stayed on stage for the full two hours, and Ronald were to expire halfway through, at 8.30 p.m., I could hardly be considered as a suspect, I reasoned.

But what if no-one should come to the concert? I had to admit that my musical tastes were not shared by everyone in the University. I therefore decided it would be prudent to arrange for a few members of the public to attend by offering them pecuniary inducements. I would never have normally considered paying people to come and hear the splendid evocation of baroque times that I am able to conjure up, but, for once, it was absolutely essential that I should have, if not a full house, certainly not an empty one.

Although feeling considerable repugnance at dear Ronald's addiction, I had recently begun to watch more closely as he administered his regular dose, and so found it quite easy to adjust this slightly and induce a deep sleep that would see him through the next two hours or so. I knew full well he didn't snore, but, as I tied him up, I also put a gag around his mouth to ensure his silence.

I had a large plastic sack handy. This was to be used for two purposes: to hide him as I carried him to the hall nearby, and to keep any blood from leaking out.

I put Ronald over my shoulder (he always was so delicate), and carried him the few yards to the back entrance of the hall just prior to the concert. This was before anyone had entered the hall, but I knew for certain that no-one would get there early. I put him into a little makeshift support I had fitted under the trapdoor, and then moved the piano in front of the trapdoor, so that it was hidden from the audience and Adrian. I tied a loop of cord around the trapdoor handle, and checked that there was enough space for me to open it with my foot.

The trapdoor was well to the left of the stage, so the piano was not obtrusive. I positioned my harpsichord slightly left of centre, and put a chair for Adrian well to the right of the stage.

With Ronald in position, I sat at my harpsichord, and awaited Adrian and my largely faithless audience.

The concert was as much a success as I had anticipated. For once, Adrian played quite well, occasionally almost as well as I, but the audience was largely unappreciative of my talent (most were clearly awaiting payment at the end of the performance). However, from my point of view, the audience was there purely to confirm my presence, and therefore fulfilled its purpose.

Halfway through the evening, we had agreed that Adrian should play a solo. I made the necessary announcements and moved away from the limelight to sit at the piano.

With the audience's attention (at least that of those still awake) firmly focused on the guitar, I was able to lift up the trapdoor by putting my left foot into the loop of cord and raising it. Then I slid over my right foot a metal ring with a long spike that I had constructed. This spike I pushed gently into Ronald's heart. All this was achieved without my moving my position at the piano more than slightly, and indeed required my glancing downwards only for a few seconds to position my feet correctly.

Prior to those actions, I had had every opportunity to back out from the plan. However, I discovered I had not felt the slightest reluctance, or even repugnance, to follow through with it.

At the end of the concert, I was immediately sought out by those who had agreed to attend in return for payment, and paid them the necessary monies (except to those who had signally failed to remain awake during the two hours, to whom I paid a much reduced fee). Strangely, I heard no comments such as "money for old rope." In fact, most seemed to feel that the payment was barely adequate for their travail.

Afterwards, I returned Ronald to our room, probably the only even-remotely risky element in my plan. I removed my additions to the trapdoor, and hid these, together with the metal foot attachment I had made and the plastic bag with which I had enshrouded Ronald. Where I hid them no one would find them.

I then telephoned the police in as agitated a fashion as I could muster.

"P.C. Plod?" I repeated.

"It's Dodd, Sir, Detective Chief Inspector." I stood corrected, but unconvinced.

To be fair, the Police, even the D.C.I. himself, had arrived very soon after my phone call. They had acted very professionally, if a little unimaginatively, but had asked most of the right questions and had done everything I had expected of them. I felt more confident.

"Looks as if he's been dead for about two hours, doesn't he?" Plod muttered. "Still we'll have to get the Doctor to confirm that."

"Yes," I asked, "Where is he?"

"He's at some do this evening. Dinner party, or something. He moves in quite high social circles, does our Dr. Mayhew. Don't worry, though: he's completely teetotal."

"Look," I said, "I don't think I can stay here with ... with Ronald. Have you any objection if I slip away and spend the night with some friends nearby?"

"That's more or less what I thought someone in your position would feel, Sir. Just give me the names and address of the folks with whom you'll be staying, in case we need to check something with you urgently. If you could just pop around to the station, the police station that is, tomorrow to make a formal statement, that should be it, I suppose."

I gave my friends' names and address, and took my leave.

I next met Plod when he called around to my rooms two days later. I had already called into the police station to give my statement, having omitted all reference to having murdered Ronald, of course, but I had expected to receive further enquiries from the D.C.I.

"The problem from our point of view, Sir," he whined, "Is that we don't have any suspects. No-one had any reason to kill Ronald Hancock, none whatsoever ... except for yourself, of course."

I surmised that he had been checking around the College, and had discovered my new relationship with Crispin, who, incidentally, was certainly not a suspect as he had been at the same dinner party as Doctor Mayhew all evening.

"But, don't forget," I countered, "I was at the concert all evening, from 7.30 p.m. until 9.30 p.m., in full view of an audience that included ..." (and here I was able to list a number of fairly eminent local people who had thankfully turned up to supplement the alibis of those I had had to pay to attend).

"Yes, yes, yes, I know," and here Plod held up his hand as if on point duty, "But Doctor Mayhew arrived straight from the dinner party at two thirty a.m., and he has stated that the deceased died between seven p.m. and nine p.m. So you see, there's no reason why you couldn't have stabbed your roommate, and *then* gone to the hall for your gig."

I spluttered, but, for once, was lost for words.

So my worst fears concerning the incompetence of the Police force had been confirmed, not, as seemed usual, to the benefit of the criminal, but robbing me of my carefully-constructed alibi.

And all because some damn fool police doctor didn't want to leave his party until it finished in the early hours of the morning, and so couldn't give anything but a vague idea of the time of death.

How do fictional murderers plan their alibis so precisely when they don't know how incompetently imprecise the police doctor is going to be?

There followed many days of my being held for questioning at the local police station. I remember I was subjected to a considerable amount of grilling, as I believe it is called.

But perhaps the Police are not quite as incompetent as I had thought.

After my being closely questioned for many days, Dodd eventually called in to see me, to admit that there had been a "little misunderstanding" in his reading of Doctor Mayhew's examination report. Because of various factors, Doctor Mayhew had been able to assess the time of death fairly accurately. In fact, my roommate must have died around 8.30 p.m., with a 45-minute margin of error.

It was unfortunate that I had only just signed a written confession.

Interval

Professor Guiteras stood up and turned to his audience.

Considering the amount of alcohol flowing around the room, he seemed surprisingly steady on his feet. Some of the students began to suspect that he was drinking more spring water than wine.

Raquel Blenkinsop was next.

She walked rather unsteadily up to Professor Guiteras, and then discovered she had left her glasses somewhere.

These were finally found under her boyfriend, and so, after several pieces of Elastoplast and Sellotape had been applied, none particularly subtly, she began.

Abracadaver

On the South coast of England, between Brighton and Bognor Regis, lies Inconton-on-Sea, a small seaside resort catering mainly for the older generations. Younger holidaymakers had started deserting the resort during the sixties and seventies as the lure of cheap package tours abroad had become stronger. For the last few years, however, the local Leisure and Amenities Department (brochure available from the Town Hall, post free) had been trying to reverse the trend, and hoped to attract the younger elements with a series of fairly ambitious publicity campaigns. These had met with varying degrees of success.

One of the more successful attempts was the rejuvenation of the 'Bijou' Theatre. Threatened with closure during the late seventies, the theatre had been reprieved by the local Council, who, rather than spend vast sums of money refurbishing the place, had instead spent the money on a public relations exercise, on appointing a "dynamic young impresario from London" as manager, and on featuring some of the best and most expensive acts available, initially it has to be said at some loss.

Now, business was booming for the 'Bijou.' Craig Swann, the new Manager, had been fairly cautious at first, staging the sort of plays put on by seaside repertory companies, but with a cast that featured someone who had once appeared in an episode of 'Coronation Street' or one of the other television soap operas. Gradually, the acts had become more prestigious, and the theatre's facilities had been improved, and now most evenings saw a packed house at the old 'Bijou.'

Except that it was now called 'Hollywood Boulevard.'

This Saturday evening's entertainment was 'A Magical Extravaganza,' starring The Stupendous Rigatoni. Craig Swann had taken into account The Stupendous Rigatoni's great popularity on television, and had pitched the price of a ticket at just the right level: the theatre was playing to a full house as usual.

The Stupendous Rigatoni (known in the business as 'Stu') was suave, handsome and debonair, and was usually attended by negligibly-attired assistants of both sexes. His great popularity was largely due to his devout following of females of all ages, but it was also due to his reputation for showing how other magicians performed their tricks (making the audience feel a part of his intimate magical world), before taking the trick one inexplicable step further, always to tumultuous applause.

Tonight was turning out to be no exception ...

"And now, ladies and gentlemen ... the very illusion that has caused the deaths of, to my reckoning, five of the greatest magicians ... two of whom were personal friends ... The Korean Bullet of Death Illusion!"

Karen Blight (stage name Stella Nova) was one of Stu's assistants that night. She wondered idly from where he had got the name. He must have just made it up, she thought, as she had never heard him or anyone else call it anything like that before. Although she was barely twenty, she had been in the business for four years already, and some of her earliest memories were of seeing some of the great magicians backstage when she was a child and her father managed a small theatre. She was brought out of her reverie as her employer continued his patter.

"For this illusion, I am going to ask the beauteous Stella here," (on cue, Stella turned, smiled, and nodded provocatively), "To fire a real bullet ... out of a real gun ... and I will catch it between my teeth!" This last phrase was said with such drama that Karen was surprised some of the more frail and elderly members of the audience didn't faint. As it was, it was obvious that most were holding their breath.

"I will need someone to come out from the audience ... to examine this very bullet ... and to inscribe it with some special mark ... so that you can *all* see it on these huge screens ... and *believe* the veracity of what follows ..."

He indicated expansively upwards towards two small screens suspended from the ceiling upon which the audience could see a closed-circuit television version of what was taking place on the stage.

A member of the audience was asked to come forward, for once, Karen noted, genuinely at random. A special 'silver' bullet was then produced with a flourish from The Stupendous Rigatoni's breast pocket, and the young girl from the audience, Debbie, a shop assistant from Gollea along the coast, marked it with as complex a pattern as she could in the limited time available. She did this in front of a small camera, and the design could clearly be seen on the screens overhead. This all took some time, during which The Stupendous Rigatoni made what he hoped would be interpreted as ethereal magical gestures.

"Thank you ... er, Lynn, was it? ... could you return to your seat please? ... thank you ... and now I shall insert the fatal bullet into the gun ... and then ... the moment of truth!" He paused for breath momentarily, and then handed the pistol to Karen. In the background, a male assistant, David Grimble, moved a sheet of glass in a frame into the middle of the stage.

"I shall ask Stella here to actually fire the gun straight at me ... through this sheet of glass here ..." (he tapped the glass to show it was real) "... and I shall catch the bullet between my teeth!"

He moved slowly and portentously across the stage, and stood on the other side of the glass panel. He took several very deep breaths, appearing to be trying to attain a trance-like state of serenity. Someone behind the scenes began a slow drum roll as Karen slowly took aim and fired directly at The Stupendous Rigatoni.

There was a gasp throughout the audience as the pistol emitted a small cloud of smoke and a loud bang, the glass screen shattered, and the magician violently shook his head and staggered backwards. He fell into a chair positioned behind him, and remained still.

It was clear that the audience hadn't quite expected such a reaction: surely he would have caught it deftly and stood smilingly with the bullet clearly held between his immaculate teeth?

It was only after a whole twenty seconds that he slowly rose to his feet, seemingly shaken by the impact. He walked to centre-stage, and then smiled to reveal the bullet between his teeth as predicted.

The whole auditorium burst into applause.

The Stupendous Rigatoni bathed in the glory for a while, and then held up his hand to quell the tumult.

"Well, that's how every other so-called magician in the business does that particular trick ... but it's only a *very* simple little trick, ladies and gentlemen ... any fool could do it ... and I'm going to show you exactly how it's done!"

This was closer to what the audience had been expecting. Perhaps The Stupendous Rigatoni had overdone things and remained still for a little too long when he had apparently caught the bullet earlier: the audience had been visibly shocked. But now the members of the audience had forgiven him and were back on his side again, as they erupted into enthusiastic applause.

"The trick is in a little sleight of hand when putting the bullet into the gun," The Stupendous Rigatoni explained, for once adopting a quiet, almost professor-like tone. "It never goes into the gun. Instead, I put into one of my many pockets, so that it can reappear magically later on."

"Of course, no-one in their right mind would expect anyone to be able to catch a speeding bullet in mid-flight, especially as most assistants, even the most beautiful ones, are pretty lousy shots, and the bullet would probably be badly deflected when passing through the glass screen. Oh, the glass screen is shattered electronically, I should add, by my assistant, Antoine, who helps me behind the scenes." From behind the scenes, David looked out and smiled.

He continued, "Then, as I apparently stumble after the bullet has been fired, I again use legerdemain to pop the little bullet into my mouth. It's so simple, n'est-ce pas?"

There was a milder ripple of applause, almost as one might expect in the more respectful ambience of a University lecture-room.

The Stupendous Rigatoni again underwent an apparent change of personality: his attitude changed to reflect the sort of enthusiasm adopted by child actors in Hollywood films of the forties who ask "Why don't we put on the show right here in the old barn?"

"So," he turned abruptly and swung his arms around almost as if he were playing golf, "Let's get the show on the road, and do the whole thing MY way."

The applause now became deafening. Even so, The Stupendous Rigatoni was a little disappointed that it wasn't just a little bit louder.

"Firstly, no disrespect to my dear friend from the audience, Carol, but not *everyone* knows her ... we need someone completely trustworthy ... and I think you know about whom I'm talking."

At a signal from him, the spotlight wavered uncertainly around the auditorium before coming to rest on a fat scruffy man just about to stuff a handful of popcorn into his capacious maw. He froze momentarily, rather as would a rabbit caught in the headlights of an approaching car, before the spotlight moved quickly to pick out the rather more august presence of his Worship the Mayor of Inconton-on-Sea sitting alongside.

He and his wife had received an invitation to attend the evening, and the Council had suggested that it would be a good thing for them to attend from the point of view of publicity. The fact that the Mayor's wife had been pestering him to buy tickets ever since the evening had been announced was immaterial.

The Mayor now stepped forward, regalia jangling, to join The Stupendous Rigatoni on stage. The magician beamed.

"Now, I have invited his, er, Worshipfulness here because he's a man you can trust, and I want you to know that there's no subterfuge going on up here."

"Firstly, let's get rid of this glass screen." He motioned to David to remove the screen to the back of the stage, before continuing, "And, so that you know that there's no way I can get hold of the bullet by trickery, I shall be standing here at the back on a stool ... so that the bullet can't travel to me through some hidden channel in the ground or by any other route except directly from the barrel of the gun!"

He asked the Mayor to examine the stool and check it for hollow legs, and then to position it wherever he liked within the area he indicated. The Stupendous Rigatoni now stood on it. Anyone watching could hardly fail to be impressed by his style and charisma. As with most great magicians, he had to continually exude charm and complete confidence in his own ability, whilst at the same time hinting at an ever-present danger and the chance that perhaps something really could go wrong.

"Now I shall remain here whilst my good friend the Mayor takes the bullet ... if you please, Stella ... and inscribes it with some personal symbol that's not too obvious ... not 'M' for Mayor, if you please, Sir! ... you can all see that being done on these television screens above, ladies and gentlemen ... could you make a few movements with your hands, your Worshipfulness, please, so that everybody knows that it's you that they're watching on the screens and not a pre-recorded tape ... thank you."

"Whilst my friend is doing that, I shall set up a small target here beside me. It's at that that Stella will be aiming. She's a qualified marksman, er, markswoman, and has been trained at Bisley, so I should be in safe hands!" Karen had actually only been to Bisley to visit an aunt, but nodded wisely.

"Obviously, I'm not daft enough to think I can catch a speeding bullet between my teeth. No-one can do that. But I *am* going to catch it in my bare hands ... if I can. Antoine, can I have the chalk, please." He plunged his hands into a box of chalk brought onto the stage by David, and covered his hands liberally with it.

"O.K. Your Worship, if you could please drop the marked bullet into the gun Stella's holding. Thank you. You can return to your seat now, if you please."

Again, The Stupendous Rigatoni began his strange breathing exercises. Karen waited patiently, gun at the ready. Although she was no markswoman, she had studied people who were good shots in readiness for this role, and looked very impressive.

"Now!"

Karen pulled the trigger, and the gun exploded into action.

The Stupendous Rigatoni shot his hands out towards the target, leapt upwards from the stool, and then spun backwards against the chair. He had already decided that he should stay motionless for perhaps a little longer this time. He had felt the audience could take perhaps thirty or forty seconds before he came around.

The audience fully expected his recovery to take some time. After all, hadn't he caught a bullet in his bare hands?

But the audience began to get restless after a whole minute had elapsed.

Then two minutes ...

Eventually, everyone in the audience, except perhaps the very oldest with poor eyesight, could discern an ever-widening trickle of blood running down from the immaculately-groomed hair of The Stupendous Rigatoni.

"I think we've strayed into John Dickson Carr territory," said Detective Chief Inspector Bloggs hopelessly. "The idea of trying to solve any murder when nothing is what it appears to be seems hopeless."

He had arrived only a few minutes after the death, and had already decided to send home all the members of the audience except the Mayor (who felt he should stay) and his wife, and two girls who said they could help. He had requested all the staff to remain, and everything to be left untouched.

"Anyway, I think I know exactly where we are, eh?" He winked at Johns, his subordinate.

Bloggs turned to those assembled in the stalls in front of him, "All right, I've heard all your stories, so now we've got to find our murderess."

Karen Blight looked indignant. "I hope that's not intended to suggest I had anything to do with it," she said.

"Oh no! You were only the one who fired the gun straight at Mr. Bland's head! You're an expert markswoman, too. Are you quite sure you haven't been involved in some kind of lover's tiff with our Mr. Bland?"

Bloggs clearly had a hatred for aliases of all types, but felt obliged to indicate the place where The Stupendous Rigatoni's body still lay covered with a blanket, as most of those assembled there seemed never to have even considered that the magician had been born with a different name. "His real name was Richard Anthony Bland."

"Look," countered Karen, "I'm no markswoman despite what Mr. Bland said, but I do help him look after the pistol, and it's never intended to actually fire a bullet. You have to maintain it well, of course. A few magicians *have* died as a result of the gun malfunctioning and actually firing the bullet. But I can assure you that the bullet didn't leave the gun this evening. It was never intended to. I don't know how, er, Mr. Bland was going to do the trick, though. He only tells us what we need to know. Sometimes he works them out on his own, sometimes he plans things with Mr. Grimble. But all he asked me to do was to fire the gun in the usual way, i.e., for it to make lots of noise and smoke, but not to actually discharge the bullet."

"Anyway, he always does a final check of the gun before his act starts. When it's your life on the line, you tend to want to double-check everything yourself."

"And he checked the gun before he went on stage tonight," she said finally.

D.C.I. Bloggs smiled humourlessly. "Then how do you explain the fact that the bullet that killed Mr. Bland was the same one that everyone saw inscribed by our Mayor, and that there was no bullet in the gun when we examined it afterwards?"

"Well, there was pandemonium after the death. Anyone on stage could have removed the bullet from the gun," piped up a voice from the stalls.

"And who might you be?" asked Detective Chief Inspector Bloggs.

The voice continued, "Oh, my name is Jean Jones. This is my friend Dilys. I asked to stay behind because I'm passionately interested in stage magic, and I feel I may be able to help. The only way in which you're going to be able to solve the murder is by understanding how the trick was intended to have been performed in the first place."

D.C.I. Bloggs was never very impressed by members of the public offering help, but, if this girl could offer some ideas or sufficient evidence to nail that Karen woman, he was willing to give her centre-stage for a few minutes.

Jean Jones continued.

"So, how was the trick to have been done? Mr. Bland could never have expected to actually catch the bullet, so it was never intended to leave the gun."

"But how did they mean to transport it from the gun to the magician's hand? We saw the Mayor inscribe the bullet and put it into the gun, all whilst Mr. Bland was on a stool at the other end of the stage."

"There is only one way in which the trick could have been engineered. The secret is often to ignore the obvious puzzle presented so enthusiastically by the magician, and try to find an alternative, perhaps unethical, solution."

"In this case, the solution is all too simple. The reason why the Mayor's inscribing his design on the bullet was shown so clearly on the overhead screens was not so much for our benefit, but for that of the assistant, Mr. Grimble, who wasn't on stage at that moment. This assistant could watch and make an almost perfect copy of the bullet. The design couldn't have been very complex as the Mayor only had a few seconds to inscribe it. "

"This bullet would then be placed near the chair behind Mr. Bland, for him to be able to pick up when he fell back."

"And that's how the trick was to have been done," Miss Jones said triumphantly.

D.C.I. Bloggs looked thoughtful, and then nodded, "Yes, it is blindingly simple, isn't it?"

Jean Jones was reminded of the way in which Sherlock Holmes' explanations of his more complex deductions were greeted by Watson.

Bloggs added, almost sulkily, "But it doesn't give me my killer, does it?"

Those in the audience who thought that Jean Jones had finished now realised that she had merely got started.

Miss Jones continued, "It's not for me, of course, to point the finger at anyone, but I do have a few ideas you might be interested in."

"Firstly, I'm certain Karen had absolutely nothing to do with the killing ..." (Bloggs muttered sotto voce "Except for pulling the bloody trigger") "... as I'm sure the gun *is* only designed for dramatic effect. Don't forget it was the same gun as she used earlier. It never left her hands during the performance, and it was certainly working well enough the first time. She has said it wasn't defective, but your Forensic Department will confirm all that. Either way, I think few would choose such a public way of murdering someone."

"Secondly, if Karen didn't shoot the fatal bullet, then the real assassin would probably have stood somewhere behind her, to incriminate her, and probably roughly in the area of the audience, to maximise the number of other potential suspects. Shooting Mr. Bland from "the wings" would have drawn attention to a far more limited number of suspects."

"Then thirdly, as no bullet was found on the chair that Mr Bland fell onto ... You didn't find one there, did you, Sir?" She looked at D.C.I. Bloggs, who shook his head. "Then thirdly, the murderer should still have the original bullet the Mayor inscribed."

"The hastily-inscribed bullet that Mr Grimble would have made would have been the one used to shoot Mr. Bland. Surely he wouldn't have faked the design and then passed it on to someone else?"

"Is Mr. Grimble a good marksman, by any chance?"

Some people might have had at least a slight feeling that, for a member of the public, this was going a little too far, but Miss Jones was now well into her stride, intoxicated with being able to act her part in a drama she could only have imagined being in before.

"Either way, for it all to work, the murderer had to get to Karen's gun after the shooting, and, in the confusion, slip the original bullet out of the gun. *That* would have had to have been a member of staff I would have thought, and, if the killer is still here, he almost certainly hasn't had a chance to dispose of it."

"That original inscribed bullet has to be here somewhere," Jean Jones said with a flourish, one she may have copied from The Stupendous Rigatoni.

"In fact, I am sure you'll still find it on Mr. Grimble, or perhaps in the box of props he manages."

D.C.I. Bloggs motioned to Johns to go and search him, but David Grimble seemed quite resigned, and came forward and volunteered the bullet.

Jean Jones nodded knowingly. "Perhaps he and Mr. Bland were the ones with the lovers' tiff!"

Interval

Professor Guiteras stood up. He was clearly irritated by a group of students talking at the back of the room.

He selected the person whom he considered was the ringleader, and asked him to tell his story next.

Harry Hubbard walked up to the front of the room.

A Hostile Reception

Hanratty House was a large office block in the City, or, rather, not too far away from it. It consisted of fourteen floors, originally all intended for the immediate occupation of some Far Eastern company that had changed its policy at the last minute and relocated elsewhere. The floors were now being occupied individually by different companies when they found that they needed to expand quickly, and, usually, only for a short period of time. Only the first six floors were currently occupied, but, nevertheless, there was still quite a crowd of office-workers in the foyer one Wednesday, waiting for the lifts to their offices.

John Burns was on duty at the reception desk that day. He watched the people waiting by the lifts, some of them only wanting to travel to the second, or even the first floor. He could never understand why the modern executive or office-worker was willing to expend so much time and money visiting health and fitness centres or buying expensive exercise machines, but felt that taking exercise in the normal course of the daily routine was beneath his or her dignity. Most executives used the car for even the shortest distance "to save time." However, this resulted in their health deteriorating because of a lack of exercise, and the solution they chose was to spend hours and a lot of money each evening working up a sweat at a health centre. If they only ignored the car more often and walked a bit more, then they probably wouldn't have to waste all that time and money, he thought. He wondered if he were missing something.

As one set of lift doors opened, those waiting to enter surged backwards, not forwards, as they usually did even if there were people trying to get out of the lift. Into the little arena thus created stumbled a short man dressed in rather smart but ageing clothes. He seemed considerably overdressed for the time of year. He stood for a few seconds, looking around as if unsure what he was expected to do, and then fell heavily to the floor clutching his chest.

John Burns was the first to reach the gentleman. He bent down and turned him over onto his back. The haft of a knife protruded from beneath the gentleman's overcoat, but he was still alive. He looked around at his audience, and said in a voice that seemed more upset than shocked, "Mr. Delahaye did it. Mr. Delahaye stabbed me." He looked around at the people gathered in the foyer. Then he closed his eyes.

A man pushed into the small group, and announced that he was a doctor. He suggested that the gentleman be carried into a small side room, where he could examine him. This done, he reappeared after a few seconds and announced that the gentleman "was no longer with us."

John Burns seemed a model witness. "I first saw the deceased, Mr. Mann I understand, when he arrived in the foyer at 0955 hours," he recounted, his words sounding vaguely regimental, but with a warmth not usually found in the armed forces. "He asked where I might find Mr. Delahaye. I told him the company was on the sixth floor, and was about to take him to the lifts, when he was met by some new employee of Delahaye's."

Detective Chief Inspector Golland interrupted him, "Had you seen this employee before?" On receiving a negative answer, he asked "Then how did you know he worked for Delahaye's?"

"Well, he was wearing Delahaye's usual blazer and trousers, and he had a Delahaye's name badge on, but I wasn't close enough to read it. I appreciate that that is hardly proof of his employment though."

"And you next saw Mr. Mann when he came out of the lift?" continued D.C.I. Golland rhetorically. "And you had never seen the doctor before? I might add that we were unable to identify or find him afterwards ..."

John Burns looked a little uncomfortable, not that any of this seemed his fault, "No, I had never seen the doctor before. But Mr. Mann had definitely been stabbed, and seemed dead, or at least very near to death, before the doctor arrived."

Penny Riddell was Lindon Mann's secretary. She said how terrible it all was, but she was either a very good secretary, well able to control her emotions in any situation, or she just didn't like him, for she seemed not particularly perturbed by the news.

"Mr. Mann phoned us here at 10.15 a.m. to say that he was actually in Mr. Delahaye's office. Perhaps I should add that he had some rather, shall we say, difficult business with two London property developers concerning some legal irregularities. The first one, David Manson, he visited a few days ago, and the second, Percy Delahaye, was on his schedule for today. He obviously felt it would be safer it we knew exactly where he was at any given time. Not that it really helped, did it?" Miss Riddell looked downcast, as if she felt she ought.

Detective Chief Inspector Golland offered his handkerchief, which was politely refused. He looked at it abstractedly, and realised it wasn't quite as clean as he would have liked. "At least we know where he was just prior to his death," he said consolingly. "You couldn't give me more details of the irregularities and of the companies involved, could you?"

Normally, each door in Barkstead Police Station had a small plaque on it announcing its function. The room in which Detective Chief Inspector Golland and one of his colleagues, Harry Ball, were talking had no plaque, probably because it wasn't large enough to be of any real use to anyone.

Arthur Golland held the floor.

"It certainly looks as if Percy Delahaye murdered Lindon Mann. Apparently, our Mr. Mann wasn't the sort of person to attract enemies, at least not recently, as it wasn't often these days that he became involved in the more contentious side of the business. There were only two people who might have had some interest in his demise: Percy Delahaye and David Manson. They both owned companies in which Mr. Mann was trying to sort out, er, irregularities, and might have been interested in keeping secrets secret."

"This morning, Lindon Mann left his office at 9.00 a.m. and walked to Hanratty House, arriving there at 9.55 a.m. We know he was met in the foyer by someone who might or might not have been an employee of Delahaye's, but who was dressed as such. He was escorted into the lift, and he was next seen emerging from the same lift with a knife sticking out of his chest, before being attended to by a doctor who materialised out of thin air, and then vanished back into it."

"Nobody in Delahaye's office admits to having seen Mann, although there is a fairly private route from the lift to Percy Delahaye's office."

"Percy Delahaye has confirmed that he had an appointment with Mann but maintains that he never turned up. He says he doesn't know why Mann would have telephoned to say he was in his office. He suggested someone might have forced him to say that."

"But even if we can't find the doctor, or the escort who met Lindon Mann, or anyone who will admit to seeing him in Delahaye's suite of offices, I think we have enough evidence to go ahead and arrest Percy Delahaye. Mr. Mann telephoned and said he was in Delahaye's office. Mr. Mann himself said it was Mr. Delahaye who had stabbed him. We've checked, and it doesn't seem likely that any other people called Delahaye might be involved. Percy Delahaye certainly doesn't have any living relatives."

"I suppose you're going to say you think David Manson did it?" he asked Harry Ball, with a look of feigned incredulity on his face.

Harry Ball was a Cornishman who had the knack of sounding as if he were actually chewing his words before he said them. He also had the knack of usually being right, which is why most people disliked him.

"Well, it certainly seems more than likely that Percy Delahaye is the man you're looking for," Harry Ball said ruminatively. "But I do have one little niggling thought."

Then he suddenly realised something.

"But hang on! All this only happened only this morning, didn't it? If there's any evidence, it might still be in Hanratty House. Do you fancy a little tour?"

At this hour of the day ten years ago, Hanratty House would have long been closed for the night. As it was, some members of staff were only just arriving as Arthur Golland and Harry Ball parked outside.

John Burns, on overtime or a different shift, was still at his desk. As he was about to finish his duty fairly soon, he offered to show the two around.

"No thank you," said Harry Ball, "We just want to have a look around, and pop up to the sixth floor to pay another visit to Delahaye's office."

John Burns nodded, "There won't be the same people there as were there earlier today, or not many of them anyway, but there should be enough folk there to show you around. I don't know about Mr. Delahaye, though. Someone said he left early this afternoon, after the interrogation."

After John Burns had indicated where the lifts obviously were, Harry Ball pressed the button and the two police officers waited for the lift.

This time there were no surprises as the lift doors opened. The two entered the lift, and Harry Ball selected the floor they required.

The lift doors opened onto a long corridor carpeted in a subtle, but no doubt hard-wearing shade of light green. The walls consisted of a number of panels, again in light green, alternate panels being emblazoned with the motif of Delahaye's. There was a small reception desk, currently unmanned. D.C.I. Golland remembered it all from his earlier visit that day.

Indeed, the whole office seemed unmanned. Although John Burns had suggested that the office would be reasonably well-staffed, there were in fact no members of staff about at all.

Harry Ball smiled.

"Look," he said, "You can wander around the place if you like, but you won't find anybody here, I'm sure. In fact, it's lucky we came here tonight, otherwise you wouldn't even have found the furniture."

His colleague continued to look a little confused, "But where is everybody? And why should they want to remove the furniture? Are you suggesting that Percy Delahaye murdered Lindon Mann, and is now about to close down his business and fly off to some far distant shore?"

Harry Ball continued to smile. He was clearly pleased with himself.

"No, no," he said, "I'm quite sure Percy Delahaye did *not* murder Lindon Mann. It's quite obvious really," he said. "Well, it is when you realise I pressed the button for the *seventh* floor."

Detective Chief Inspector Golland had always hated the ending to the old Perry Mason series, where Perry and his staff sat around in a group, and someone asked, "But, Perry, how did you know he was the murderer?" It was all so contrived, he felt.

He now found himself in almost exactly the same position. He asked Harry Ball how he had worked out what had really happened.

Harry sat back in the only comfortable chair in the unnamed room at the police station.

"Well, Perry," he said grinning, "It did all seem a little too contrived and, well, stagy, I suppose you'd call it. But there were a few questions that needed answering."

"Where did the escort come from, and why did the doctor vanish so efficiently? Why did the doctor arrive exactly on cue: was it to allow Mr. Mann to say enough to incriminate Percy Delahaye and no more? If Mr. Delahaye had stabbed poor Mr. Mann, why did he allow him to escape so easily, bearing in mind that he was badly injured? Why should he try to kill him when he almost certainly knew Mr. Mann had already said where he was on the telephone to his secretary?"

"Surely, someone as resourceful as a successful property developer would have realised that there were only two likely suspects, and arranged to have the finger pointed at the other ... or had the other potential suspect already decided to do that?"

"So, was it possible that David Manson could have murdered Lindon Mann and made it look almost indubitably as if it were his rival to blame?"

"I *could* think of one way, and so I put it to the test this evening, with the results that you saw."

Arthur Golland coughed, "So what exactly were the results that I saw?"

"David Manson must have learnt of Lindon Mann's appointment. He probably told him himself at their recent meeting. He arranged for one of his employees to meet Lindon Mann in the foyer of Hanratty House. In the lift, this escort then pressed the button for the seventh, not the sixth, floor. He would have kept this well-hidden from Mr. Mann."

"I'm sure any property developer could have turned part of this empty floor into an apparently-flourishing and efficient-looking office in a few hours, and Manson had a few days' notice. Lindon Mann had probably visited Delahaye's a few times, but would hardly have noticed or bothered about the inevitable slight differences."

"Of course, I don't know the minute details, but I imagine that this escort probably told Lindon Mann that Percy Delahaye was slightly delayed, but that his (non-existent) relative, another Mr. Delahaye, would entertain him until Percy arrived. If no Christian names had been given, "Mr. Delahaye" would have been the only name Mann would have known him by. And so, in the presence of this 'relative,' it was with this name that he described the office to his secretary when he telephoned her. David Manson would have known of Mann's policy of telephoning his movements when visiting 'difficult' people from his visits to his own office, no doubt."

"And so, after a far from fatal stabbing, he was able to tell the onlookers that it was indeed Mr. Delahaye who had stabbed him."

"And it was then up to the bogus doctor to finish him off on cue."

Interval

Jean Lewis really should not have been left until so near the end of the evening. It was not often that she had the chance to drink some of the better-quality wines, and she was now making up for this with noticeable enthusiasm.

She stumbled rather clumsily to her feet, and lurched gracelessly towards the Professor.

She cleared her throat, once quietly, then once again with greater sonority, before starting to speak.

Although her unsteady actions clearly indicated the large amount of alcohol she had consumed, when she began her story, she spoke with greater eloquence than many of the more sober story-tellers that evening.

Grotesquerie

The small contingent of policemen was met in the foyer of the hotel by its manager.

"Welcome to The Endeavor Genuine Elizabethan Manor Hotel, Gentlemen," he intoned in a mid-Atlantic accent that was difficult to place. "I hope you have been professionally impressed with our security arrangements."

Indeed, it had taken the hapless policemen a considerable amount of time to prove their identities and gain admittance to the hotel, and this despite all but the Detective Chief Inspector being in full uniform and the group having arrived in two clearly-marked police cars.

The manager waved his arms expansively around the large foyer. "Our American parent company, the Quainte Olde Charme Hotels Conglomerate bought this genuine Elizabethan manor only two years ago, but have already imposed every conceivable security feature upon the establishment, as you have witnessed."

"All the original walls have been removed and carefully stored for posterity. The interior walls have been replaced with high-security, bomb-retardant, synthetic wood-panelling. The exterior walls have been replaced with new structures that can withstand a tank attack. Boy, did we all enjoy testing that out!"

"As to the glazing, we have now installed reproduction-style poly ... er, polyscientific windows that totally rule out entry or egress."

"So all visitors must use this main foyer, with security guards on duty twenty-four hours a day." He smiled.

The D.C.I. asked, "So all that's left of the original Elizabethan manor are the foundations?"

The manager should have squirmed, but nodded proudly and smiled.

"We were established specifically for the accommodation of corporate functions, and we cater to practically every large company in the Midlands, providing the best accommodation, the hautest cuisine, and the most safe and secure environment. In the corporate minds of our clients, Security is the most important of the services we provide."

The manager brought his introductory speech to a none-too-hasty conclusion, "So, whilst we regret the unpleasantness of last night, I trust that, having applied such rigorous security measures, we may have assisted you in containing the problem, and hopefully in pointing you in the direction of an early solution."

Detective Chief Inspector Lewis thanked the manager as ungratefully as he could, and asked if he could interview the last people to have spoken to the very-recently-deceased Mrs. Dunn. The manager nodded obsequiously, and led him to Mr. and Mrs. White, who were sitting in a corner of the main lounge in eager anticipation of this promised interview.

Mr. and Mrs. White were two elderly people who obviously relished a good story, especially if they could be at the centre of it. They spoke alternately almost as if there were a relay baton being constantly passed between them. Their two narratives fused easily into one.

"Well, we had met Mr. and Mrs. Dunn, such nice people, before at Chandler Inc's Traditional Annual Dickensian Christmas Hoedown here last October. Such a nice couple, and so well-suited too. Anyway, when Donald and Deirdre turned up this year, they seemed ill at ease. They argued quite a lot, and a Melanie was mentioned. Well, Donnie left us for a few minutes, so we were able to have a good chinwag with Deirdre, and she confirmed that things weren't going too well."

"Then she found Donnie actually dancing with this Melanie, and there was a terrible row, not a good thing in front of all the bosses, what with so much redeployment and relocation going on within the company. I mean, thank goodness I retired from the old company before it was taken over and became efficient."

D.C.I. Lewis nodded. He idly wondered why they had been invited to a function organised by such an obviously thrusting and unsentimental company. He thought they probably still had a friend in the secretary's office, otherwise their names would have been left off the list years ago. He wasn't too sure why they still wanted to attend though.

"So there was this huge row, and Deirdre and this Melanie almost came to blows. She was wearing lots and lots of makeup, her peroxide blonde hair was piled high, and she had on a very small low-cut mini-dress that beautifully showcased her collection of tattoos: I mean, Deirdre looked fantastic. We don't know what Donnie saw in this Melanie, who had dark hair and had clearly never had any cosmetic surgery. Anyway, things cooled down for a while, but, when we saw Deirdre later, she was on her own and looking distraught. She was wringing her hands just as someone would do in a film. She said it was because of Donnie. He'd taken this Melanie up to her room, I mean, to Melanie's room. Deirdre had gone to reception and found out which room it was. That surprised us, as we had had enough trouble trying to find out our own room number. Then she seemed to make up her mind what to do, and stormed upstairs. The door was not far from the top of the staircase, and we could see and hear what was going on from the foyer. Deirdre pounded on the door and demanded to be let in. Even though she yelled that she could hear them inside, they didn't open the door. The way Deirdre was acting, I wouldn't have either."

"Then she came back downstairs and said she was going to find out what was going on if it was the last thing she ever did. Which was odd, because it was obvious to everyone else what was going on." Here, Mr. White sniggered, which oddly rather shocked the Detective Chief Inspector.

"And it *was* the last thing she ever did! She stormed into the foyer, collected her pass from the security people (otherwise she would never have got back in again), and stamped out into the garden. We thought she just wanted to have a walk around to clear her head, but, on reflection, I suppose it was rather too cold for that."

The previous evening, Gordon Jobson had had similar ideas. Having realised that he had drunk rather too much of some overpriced Californian Bordeaux, he had decided that it would be wise to try and clear his head in the gardens, especially as he was also feeling rather sick, and didn't wish to mess up his chances of promotion by staying in the hotel.

And he had stumbled upon the body of Deirdre Dunn.

"I don't know where I wandered at first, but things became a little clearer afterwards, and I found myself in front of the hotel. Then I turned onto a path parallel to the west side of the hotel, where it begins to drop slightly until you enter a little gorge, I suppose you might call it. It's just basically a little cutting where the path dips well below the level of the ground, and it's lined with rough stones. It looks very natural, but I doubt whether it is. Nothing seems natural here, although the Americans probably think it is. It's all about as authentic as those London film sets in old Hollywood movies."

"I suppose the gorge would be nice and cool in the summer, but not on a cold wintry night. That's where I found Mrs. Dunn. She was lying on the path below the steep stone walls. I could see blood coming from a wound on her head." Gordon Jobson's head had obviously cleared up now, as he anticipated the next question. "I could just about make things out, as there was a small floodlight they'd set up between the rocks. I think it was all meant to be romantic."

Gordon Jobson had been interviewed as he walked with the D.C.I. towards the gorge. As they arrived there, D.C.I. Lewis thought it would be hard to feel romantic in such a cold, even clammy, place, but the presence of several police barriers, a temporary incident hut, and the usual paraphernalia of police scene-of-crime investigation wouldn't have helped. Neither did knowing there was a dead body at the centre of it all. There wasn't a lot of space down in the gorge, so D.C.I. Lewis decided to send some of the constables to find out if anyone else in the hotel had anything of interest to say and whether anyone had any obvious connections with the dead woman. Donnie Dunn he would interview himself later.

The Forensic people were still in the little gorge. Dr. Bodger had now arrived, and appeared to have completed his preliminary investigations.

"She hit her head on a large rock, probably one of those around here," Dr. Bodger said, waving his arms around in a rather vague fashion. "There are a few pieces of earth around the wound, and they seem to match the soil here. I don't think she could have merely fallen from the rocks above though, as there seems to have been rather more force involved than that. I suppose she could have been thrown from the top, or violently pushed ..."

And that seemed to be all he would say before a laboratory examination.

Lewis looked up at the rocks above. "Is there a quick way up to there?" he asked.

The manager suddenly materialised alongside. "If you would care to follow me, I can show you the shortest route," he said, helpfully for once.

The manager led them back towards the entrance to the hotel, and then along a paved terrace along the west side of the hotel.

The terrace lay on three sides of the hotel, and was bordered by a stone balustrade. The stonework looked well-worn and ancient, but Lewis thought he had seen something very similar, although rather less synthetically-weathered, at his local garden centre the previous weekend. On the other side of the balustrade, the manager indicated, there was a short slope and then the rocks at the top of 'The Grotto.'

D.C.I. Lewis, however, was more interested in an old bucket and some ropes well-hidden on the other side of the stone balustrade. "Have you still got the builders in?" he enquired.

The manager obviously felt embarrassed that any such eyesore should form a blemish against the pure, if uncompromisingly bland, facade of his establishment, "Oh no!" he stuttered, "The workmanship around here is terrible. We had these special windows, poly, er ... you remember, I told you about them ... flown in from America, but they were installed by local people, and they've started to leak in places. I had to hire specialists from Reading, or Norwich, ... or somewhere in London anyway ... and they're trying to correct the problem, but I think the firm just sub-contracted to another local company, because the workmen don't seem very professional. It's taking them considerably longer than I would have expected, even though we're paying them to work evenings too. There always seem to be tools and ropes lying everywhere, even though I keep reminding the men about the danger to guests."

"Where would Mr. Dunn's room be?" asked the D.C.I.

"Oh, on the other side of the hotel," replied the manager, who would probably not have normally known where any of his guests were staying.

"Hang on," countered the D.C.I., "No, what I should be asking is where Miss, er ... Melanie's room is."

"*Mrs*. Melanie Parker's room would be on the first floor directly above us now," the manager said.

"The problem as I see it," rambled Detective Chief Inspector Lewis, "Is that we have a woman, almost certainly murdered, lying at the bottom of some damn-fool artificial love-cave ..." he seemed to be struggling for the most apt, if not disdainful, adjectives, "... and only one person, or two persons if you include Mrs. Melanie Parker, with the motive to kill her, and both of them upstairs in a hotel bedroom at the time of her death."

"The security measures seem designed to monitor everyone's movements, and to stifle any possibly antisocial activities which anyone might feel tempted to indulge in. Anyway, we know that the late Mrs. Dunn left the hotel at 21.14 (they logged 211422!), and that her husband remained within the building all night, at least until the body was found. Mr. Dunn spent most of the time in Melanie Parker's room, as indeed did Mrs. Parker."

"I've interviewed both Mr. Dunn and Mrs. Parker, and both claim not to have seen Mrs. Dunn after they had entered Mrs. Parker's bedroom, although they admit that they heard her hammering on the door and yelling soon afterwards."

"There are cameras in all the main corridors ... probably in the bedrooms as well, for all we know ... and the security people have checked the tapes and are positive neither Dunn nor Parker left the room until after Jobson ran screaming into Reception to tell them of his find."

"Those rooms are almost hermetically sealed. The windows open a few inches, and that's that. You can open them fully in the case of fire, but then you can't reset them, so Mr. Dunn couldn't have left the room at all."

"It's a pity she wasn't shot. You could have fired through that gap in the windows, and there are two beautiful long-barrelled antique guns mounted on the wall, and the manager assures me they actually work."

P.C. Bone sat thoughtfully for a moment.

Finally, he said, "I have an idea that Mrs. Dunn did what any self-respecting wronged wife would do under the circumstances."

"I suggest we try and find some of those workmen. The manager said he's asked them to work on the other side of the estate for a few days so as not to get involved in all this."

They eventually tracked down a small group of workmen drinking tea in an old caravan hidden within a small circle of trees near the back of the hotel.

P.C. Bone took the initiative, probably because his superior seemed unsure what to ask, "We're looking for anyone who saw anything unusual around the west side of the hotel last night. Were any of you gentlemen working the evening shift?"

The scruffiest, yet oldest, member of the group assumed the role of spokesman. "We were all working yesterday evening, but on the east side, as that was the only area where we had any work we could do quietly. The manager insisted on that, but I don't know why, because there was such a racket coming from the ballroom that we could hardly concentrate." He nodded in the direction of one of the workmen who was part of a small group studiously playing cards in a corner, "Crispin went to the west side after we left, to tidy up, didn't you?"

Crispin looked a little unsure, probably trying to work out where north was, but then nodded, "Aye, I was there to clear things up after the rest of you lot left at nine. There wasn't much there, but the manager here insists that nothing is left lying around at any time, in case some of his precious clients hurt themselves. But I hardly saw a soul, and I certainly didn't see anything suspicious or I would have reported it."

"And was there anything left that you had to tidy up?"

Crispin again looked unsure, but P.C. Bone decided that this might be his natural mien. "Well, there were a few boxes and other impedimenta." The two detectives assumed this to be his token long word.

P.C. Bone prompted him, "And who asked you to move the ladder? Did he say you'd get into trouble if you didn't?"

Crispin looked a little taken aback. He hesitated for a few seconds, and then continued, "Yes, there was some bloke in an upstairs window. He asked me to move the ladder far away before somebody fell over it. He seemed reasonable at first, but then he said if anybody got to hear of it, I'd be in hot water, so I'd better not mention it to anybody."

"And you'd recognise this bloke again were you to meet him?" enquired Bone.

Crispin answered yes, yes, quite definitely.

Having decided not to take advantage of the hotel's stylish, but supremely uncomfortable, seating, P.C. Bone and D.C.I. Lewis were sitting outside on some steps.

"Mrs. Dunn left the hotel that night in a blind fury," P.C. Bone explained to D.C.I. Lewis. "The one thing uppermost in her mind was to get proof of her husband's infidelity."

His superior countered with, "Or perhaps she just wanted to catch them at it." He smiled uncharacteristically.

P.C. Bone ignored him. "So she leaves the hotel, perhaps to clear her head for a moment. Possibly without thinking, she finds herself under the window where her husband is. And there in front of her is a discarded ladder."

"She puts the ladder up against the wall to look through the window, but her husband sees her. Angrily, he tries to open the window, but can only open it a few inches ... just enough, in fact, to be able to push the ladder ..."

"... probably using one of those long-barrelled guns in the room," added Lewis, clearly trying to justify his earlier thoughts about the weapons.

"So the ladder tilts backwards, with Mrs. Dunn hanging on, and she's flung over the balustrade down towards 'The Grotto.' If the ladder were only a bit longer than the width of the terrace, it wouldn't follow her into the gorge, but would remain lying on the terrace ... until, that is, and no doubt to Mr. Dunn's great relief, a workman appears. That meant he wouldn't have to leave the hotel to move the ladder."

Detective Chief Inspector Lewis thought for a few seconds, "And if we can get that workman to confirm that it was indeed Mr. Dunn who called out from that window, we should have a case."

Interval

There now followed one of the most unfortunate incidents of the evening. One female student who had already given her story chose that moment to become violently sick, unfortunately over a girl with whom she shared a mutual dislike.

This was then followed by the accusation that the various projectiles had in fact been aimed, rather than allowed to choose their target at random.

The resulting argument and fight took far longer to clear up than did the carpet.

Professor Guiteras tried as well as he could to defuse the situation, but his attempts at appeasement did not pacify the two girls. Indeed the situation was deteriorating rapidly when a young man rose from the back of the room and offered to tell his story.

He was clearly popular with both the girls (indeed one wonders whether he might have been the cause of the mutual dislike in the first place).

The two girls sat back meekly and listened.

John James began his story.

A Surfeit of Shoes

Even though Mr. Blooper had died almost a year ago, George Benson still went for his early morning walk at 5.30 a.m., as he had done with at least three previous dogs. Before his retirement, he had worked on the early shift at a small factory in East London for over forty years, and always woke at 5.00 a.m., whether or not he'd set his alarm clock.

Even when he had had a dog with him, he had always spent most of the time looking at the Thames, examining the bits of wood, plastic bags, and other detritus that floated upon its surface, trying to identify something either valuable or sensational. Already this morning, he had spotted a small tiara, a severed leg, and two complete human bodies, one of which bore an uncanny resemblance to Lord Lucan. Even though all of these had turned out, upon closer inspection, to be extremely uninteresting, it still confirmed Mr. Benson's opinion that it was a lot more exciting walking here than in the local park. As he reached the old grain warehouse and turned back towards his house, he spotted something in the water that turned out to be rather more interesting than his previous finds ...

"So, how long had he been in the water?" asked Detective Chief Inspector Farr.

"Since about early yesterday evening between six and nine, I'd say," replied Detective Box, his current subordinate, although they changed surprisingly frequently. "I worked the riverside beat for a while, so I'm pretty good at estimating, but I wouldn't like to contradict the good doctor here." This last clause was added because of the close proximity of the good doctor, who was painstakingly examining the body, which had by now been disengaged from the floating debris with which it had become entangled, and had been pulled up onto the side of the small lane in which they were standing. The good doctor seemed not to be in a hurry.

The body was that of a fairly elderly man, aged around seventy. He was dressed in clothes that had probably once been moderately expensive: a brown jacket with brown (but not quite matching) trousers, a white shirt, and a brown tie, but no shoes.

"He has a few small injuries, but nothing he might not have got whilst in the water. There's certainly nothing inconsistent with this being an accident or a suicide. However, I doubt he could have put up much of a fight anyway." The body certainly did look very frail: although around five feet ten, the frame was very slight. The Doctor finished with "That's all for the moment. I'll give you a full report as soon as I can."

"We know who he was, anyway," said Box. "The papers in his pocket were pretty waterlogged, but he had name tags on all his clothes, and he had a credit card too, thank God, so we've been able to trace his address."

"O.K.," said D.C.I. Farr, heading towards his car, "Let's see if he's in. It's bloody cold here, and I'm getting fed up anyway."

Mafeking Terrace had clearly been built when the name was on everybody's lips, or at least within recent living memory. "It must be a relief road," murmured Box. Once a sorry, sad street of brown terraced houses, their value had increased rapidly over the last few decades, and both sides of the road were now lined with expensive and mostly brand-new cars. Only number 39 seemed to have preserved its original dull aspect, and it was here that the recently-deceased Arthur Morton had lived.

"That was quick," said an ancient head that looked out of the doorway of number 37 as they rang the bell. "You are from the Police, aren't you?" it asked.

"Er, yes, we are," said D.C.I. Farr, a little worried that it might be so obvious.

"Well, I only telephoned you a few minutes ago. Arthur has been out all night. He dropped his key in, as he usually does when he goes out, at four yesterday afternoon, and he hasn't called in to collect it yet."

"Perhaps you had better let us in to have a look around," said Box, proffering his identification, although it was hardly glanced at.

The interior of the house was as bereft of colour as the outside.

Mrs. Betty Wright, as she announced herself to be, sat on the sofa. Her eyesight must have been fairly poor, otherwise she would have noticed a typewritten envelope propped up in the centre of the table and enquired about its contents. The two policemen decided to ignore it until she had left.

"Four o'clock it was he left yesterday afternoon. I know it was four because 'Tea with Biskit' was just starting on television. I asked where he was going to, of course - I mean, at his age, it's as well to keep track of people, isn't it? - and he said he was going to meet his Uncle Albert, but he had a sly sort of smile on his face as he said it. But it's nice to see Arthur going out a bit more these days. His wife died from cancer only six months ago. He's only got his daughter now, but she doesn't call in much ... and when she does, it's never for long."

Mrs. Wright continued in the same vein for some time, despite an official silence and a total lack of encouragement from her audience. The rest of her monologue, all of which was totally unrelated to the case, was indeed of little interest to anyone under the age of sixty-five.

After a while, D.C.I. Farr felt obliged to interrupt Mrs. Wright, thank her for her help, and request his subordinate to show her out. "You'd better leave the key with us," he added. When Box returned, D.C.I. Farr had already read the short note in the envelope.

The envelope had "To Whom It May Concern" typed on it, a quite ancient typewriter having obviously been used: that in the corner of the room would almost certainly be proved to be the one. Inside was a single sheet of paper torn from a spiral notepad, the sort that stationery companies believe reporters always use. Two lines right at the top of the page simply said, "I can't go on. It will have to be Chiswick Bridge." Chiswick would be the nearest bridge to Mafeking Terrace, Farr thought.

There was little enough of interest to anyone in the rest of the house, so the two left and sat in the car for a while to discuss things.

After a few moments, the car's communication system began to emit strange bleeping noises. Box grabbed the handset, and listened for a while.

"We'll be right there," he answered finally, and then turned to Farr.

"They've found what they think are Mr. Morton's shoes on Chiswick Bridge, and they'd like them identified."

The shoes had been found by a constable patrolling the bridge at "oh eight hundred hours" (it had actually been five past eight, but the constable wasn't sure how to phrase that). He had seemed so pleased with himself on the telephone that Box rather suspected they might find him waiting for them in the middle of the road, waving the shoes in the air triumphantly. But thankfully the usual procedures had been followed, and the shoes were as they had been found, untouched. They had been placed well away from the roadway, up against the balustrade of the bridge, but in full view, and lined up rather neatly.

The shoes themselves were clearly once quite expensive, but were now rather elderly and much-used. They were grey, with elasticated gussets, but it would be difficult to trace from where they had been bought, as the brand name inside the shoes had long been worn away.

Box, who had once been a traffic policeman, said something to the effect that he reckoned that they had done about four hundred miles, and only had about half-a-millimetre of tread left, but was only rewarded with a smileless stare from his boss.

Inside the shoes was written the owner's name in biro. Box thought it rather an old-fashioned idea to identify one's property so carefully, but it was probably the sort of habit one gained at school, or in the Army, and kept for the rest of one's life. The name seemed to have been worn away at least once, but had been re-written: the name was clearly 'Arthur Morton,' and the name had equally clearly been in the shoes for some time.

"There's something that worries me about these shoes ... even apart from the fact that the colour doesn't match that of the clothes Mr. Morton was wearing when we found his body," Box muttered.

"I think I know what you're thinking," said Farr, who for once really did.

Neither Farr nor Box fancied spending too much time on the bridge, so they had just finished giving instructions to the constable and a colleague who had been summoned, when Farr exclaimed, "Ah, here's a likely-looking candidate!"

There is a vast army of London homeless that lives in the area and crosses the various bridges in London every day. Most of them seem to be evicted fairly early in the morning from wherever they had found to sleep that night, and so even those who had crossed the bridge late last night or in the early hours might still be found returning over the bridge at this hour of the morning.

D.C.I. Farr had instructed the constables to interview any such vagrants. They were to ask if any of them had crossed the bridge during the preceding fourteen hours or so, and, if so, had they passed the spot where the shoes were found, and had they seen them there?

It was Farr and Box's contention that, had such a smart pair of shoes been left openly on the bridge early the previous evening, then surely some vagrant would have taken them during the fourteen hours or so that had elapsed before the constable found them that morning.

Farr's likely-looking candidate was now shuffling his way across the bridge. His attire was too old and tattered even to be considered for recycling, and even the piece of string holding up his trousers was threadbare. However, his brown shoes looked very smart and well-cared-for.

It took some time before this gentleman was willing to open up about from where he had obtained his smart shoes.

He initially said he had had the shoes for some months. However, upon examining the shoes, the name 'Arthur Morton' was clearly inscribed inside.

It took a long conversation involving threats of "visiting the station," and the promise of a new pair of shoes to replace the "evidence" he was wearing, before the scruffy gentleman (christened Porter Latimer Vaughan-Phillips, not that that matters) finally became more open.

"Well, I was crossing Chiswick Bridge around two o'clock this morning. There was this pair of shoes there, but clearly nobody wanted or needed them, and *I* did, so I took them."

"Did you see any other shoes there?" Box added.

The vagrant looked a bit surprised at that question. "Definitely not. There was only the one pair."

A statement had had to be taken, despite protestations from the vagrant. D.C.I. Farr asked one of the constables to take him along to the Station.

"What about those new shoes you promised?" asked the scruffy gentleman.

D.C.I. Farr slipped the constable a few pound coins and asked him to get something from a charity shop.

The vagrant looked rather crestfallen.

Box and Farr sat in their unmarked police car parked within sight of the bridge (one of the perks of being in the Force was that you could park just about anywhere).

Farr spoke first.

"So, why on earth *would* someone intent on suicide need to have two pairs of shoes?"

"Maybe he didn't want to get the first pair dirty," volunteered Box.

"So, what have we got? Arthur Morton entered the River Thames at some time yesterday evening between six and nine o'clock. At around two in the morning, a pair of his brown shoes was found on Chiswick Bridge and appropriated by our vagrant. Around four hours later, around six o'clock, Mr. Morton is fished out of the Thames. Then, at eight a.m., another pair of his shoes, this time in grey, is found in almost exactly the same spot as the first."

Farr stared through the car windscreen vacantly, clearly trying to think. There was a slight whirring noise, but Box soon realised that this was caused by a defective heater motor, not the inside of Farr's head.

Box had a knack of saying things just before they became strangely relevant. "One thing that worries me a little is that the neighbour said that Arthur Morton had started "going out a bit more these days." She may have been referring only to last night, or perhaps one visit to the local Senior Citizens' Hall might have seemed extravagant to her. But she seemed to think he'd begun to get over his wife's demise in a way that perhaps wasn't consistent with suicide."

Here he was interrupted, as the radio equipment again made strange bleeping noises. He listened for a few seconds, then whistled and raised his eyebrows.

"Arthur Morton's fiancée has just contacted the Station. He was getting married in five weeks' time."

Farr mused for a moment, then said, "I think I'd rather like to go and see the daughter first though. I wonder whether she has an alibi."

Melissa Morton did indeed have an alibi. They interviewed her at her house, which was situated in a quiet mews not too far from her father's house, but in a better area, on the other side of the Thames.

Clearly a career-conscious (if not career-obsessed) person, she had spent the whole of the preceding day at a conference for the company she worked for. This had taken place in the company's London headquarters, a large block of converted riverside warehouses just to the east of the Tower of London. As with many such conferences these days, it seemed designed to allow (or demand?) employees to demonstrate their total commitment to the company by starting early in the morning and continuing well into the evening, before a night of 'optional' convivial hospitality. She herself had left after one o'clock ("It's O.K. I restricted myself to just the one bottle of wine as I was driving" - Box winced). During this time, she said she had left the function room for no more than ten or fifteen minutes on a small number of occasions, to "check on a few facts on the spreadsheets, powder my nose, or generally do some checking up on people on-line."

She seemed drained, but this appeared to be as a result of the all-day conference, as she didn't seem very shocked about her father. She said he had lost most of his interest in life, and so she wasn't too surprised, and, well, did they know his wife had died fairly recently?

D.C.I. Farr thought she'd probably have a good cry when she was alone, but then decided she probably wouldn't.

Almost as an afterthought, D.C.I. Farr said, "We're trying to confirm his movements yesterday evening. Mrs. Betty Wright, his neighbour, said he had intended visiting his Uncle Albert. Have you got his address by any chance?"

Melissa Morton was very well-organised. She turned to her computer on the desk beside her, and entered Uncle Albert's name.

"Oh," said Melissa Morton slowly. "Uncle Albert died three years ago."

Once again, the two were sitting in the car talking. Neither felt like returning to the Station, and it was too cold to be outside. Furthermore, there was a current blitz on drinking whilst on duty, so the pub across the road was out of bounds unless they felt like a mineral water each.

"I have to say," said D.C.I. Farr, "That I don't like Miss Morton very much, and I wouldn't put it past her to murder her own father. However, she has an alibi, and the death may very well have been a suicide."

Box was also in a contemplative mood. "I agree that she seems, if not culpable, certainly more than capable."

Most of the other boring tasks had now been done that afternoon by various members of the Force. Both pairs of shoes had been confirmed as having been owned and worn at some time or other by Mr. Morton. His time of death was confirmed as between six and eight p.m. The fiancée, Dorothy Bullock, had been interviewed: she hadn't seen "her Arthur" for three days, and had a watertight alibi. Melissa Morton's alibi had been confirmed: she hadn't moved out of the spotlight at the conference for more than ten to twenty minutes at any time.

"So, we have only one real suspect, and she was a considerable distance downstream of Chiswick Bridge all evening and an hour or so into the morning," said D.C.I. Farr.

"Right, let's go over what we've got, summarise the evidence, and come up with some theories as to what actually happened to the deceased."

D.C.I. Farr for once sounded quite purposeful, as if he were totally in charge of the situation. Then his confidence seemed to wane, and his voice become a little more pleading, "And why do we have an elderly gentleman in a possibly suicidal frame of mind who insists on wearing two pairs of shoes?"

"Let's assume it *was* suicide," theorised Box. "Arthur Morton leaves a suicide note, and jumps off Chiswick Bridge between six and eight p.m., apparently leaving his shoes where he jumped. These are unnoticed until two a.m., when our vagrant crosses the bridge and finds only *one* pair, which he takes. So, why did no-one spot the second pair of shoes until Constable, er, whoever he was, finds them at eight a.m.?"

"Even if Arthur Morton had put them in different places on the bridge, I'm sure some itinerant would have found the second pair before eight in the morning. So, one pair of shoes must have been put on the bridge before around two a.m., but the second pair almost certainly was put there later, probably much later. If so, someone else *must* have been involved, and it looks more like murder."

"If it's murder, then we really only have one suspect, who was at a conference during the time the deceased died. Our dear Melissa couldn't have been at Chiswick Bridge much before 2.00 a.m. ..."

Box continued, brightening, "... when she *could* have deposited the first pair of shoes on the bridge ..."

After a few seconds, Box finished the sentence, "... on her way to her father's house to prepare the previously-concocted suicide note."

Farr mused, "I can imagine her putting out a new telephone pad a few days previously, and then telephoning her father, pretending to be a friend with an urgent message about her car breaking down and having to meet Melissa on Chiswick Bridge. No doubt she would adopt a very brisk businesslike attitude and force him to take down the message verbatim, "Look, take this down word for word, and give it to Melissa." Yes, having met her, I can imagine that all too clearly. With Melissa as a daughter, I imagine he was quite used to taking orders."

Box was becoming more confident, "And on the way back over Chiswick Bridge, if she saw that the first pair of shoes had gone, or perhaps if she actually saw them walking off, as it were, what should she do? Risk chasing the vagrant and trying to persuade him to return them? Even if she could catch him, that could create an unnecessary fuss. No, I think she'd probably decide that they were gone for ever, and that no-one would ever find them again. She'd return to Mafeking Terrace and find another easily-identifiable pair, and then wait until she could leave them on the Bridge just as our constable was approaching around eight a.m."

"That's an awful lot of to-ing and fro-ing and waiting. Would it all be worth it?" muttered Farr.

Box had now thought it all out. "It would if it were imperative that Chiswick

Bridge were confirmed as the place from where Arthur Morton had jumped."

"What if she had actually drowned him at her office near the Tower?"

Farr appeared to be chewing all this over in his mind, so Box filled in the gaps for him.

"She could have arranged to meet her father near to her offices, perhaps to discuss his forthcoming marriage or to visit Dorothy Bullock together. To fit in with the clandestine air, she must have suggested that her father say he was going to see Uncle Albert. She must have known that he had passed away, adding to the impression that her father was considering suicide, and the whimsicality might have appealed to her father."

"Her offices are right alongside the Thames. She merely had to stun him, remove his shoes to plant later, and drop him into the river. There may even be some easy means of access to the water from her offices."

It was as Farr and Box were on their way to Melissa Morton's place of work that they received a phone call from the Forensics team that Farr has asked to examine the riverside by her offices. Certain of Miss Morton's garments had been removed from her house (legally, but under considerable protest), and the team had been able to match mud samples from the clothes with that found by the Thames. Fibres from both Melissa's clothes and her father's were also found and matched.

There were also signs of a very small struggle.

Interval

Professor Guiteras' decision to ask John James to read had been successful, at least for the duration of his story.

Almost immediately after he had returned to his seat, after only the briefest of lulls, the two girls began arguing again.

This time, it took twenty minutes to calm everyone down.

This was mostly due to the intervention of Michelle Russell, who had done some work for the Samaritans (although her stint there had been largely unsuccessful in terms of the ratio of her successes to her failures).

Professor Guiteras therefore decided that Michelle should give the next story, though this was probably not taken as a compliment. She had been dreading the moment all evening, and was nervous almost to the point of incoherence.

Foul Whisperings

John and Deborah (never, never Debbie) felt quite relaxed in the airport departure lounge, even though their flight to Australia had been delayed by two hours.

They were sitting in one corner overlooking the runway, whilst the few other people in the sparsely-populated lounge were some distance away, certainly not within earshot.

"Don't worry, Deborah, they won't come looking for us. As soon as we're in Oz, we can forget everything and make a fresh start. We've got enough money to do that now, anyway."

"I'm not worried, John. We've got no criminal record, I don't think we left any real clues, and we're leaving the country before anyone can connect us with it all."

"Anyway," she continued, "It was only a couple of burglaries - eighteen, nineteen? - and a few old ladies who got in the way."

"Yeah, they seem to fight more than younger people. People our age just seem to accept it as a fact of life - especially if they're insured, anyway - but the oldies seem to take it as a personal insult and feel they have to try and stop you."

Deborah smiled and looked into John's face, "They didn't stop you, Darling, did they?"

"You know, I doubt if the authorities would even realise it was anything other than an accident, at least at the Vicarage and that old cottage by Almington. They'd know it was a burglary, of course, but those stupid cops would probably think the old dears fell down the stairs trying to run after us! Housebreaking is so much better in the country. In town, they've got nosy neighbours, alarms, lots of police stations … but, in small villages, there's nothing."

"As long as they haven't got big dogs," Deborah reminded him, as he winced.

"But not many old ladies have got anything other than a little poodle or," smiling, "A pussy cat."

It was Deborah's turn to wince.

She had started getting a little edgy now, thought John. He had expected this of her, as she wasn't quite as hard as he was, and he thought she might start feeling a little anxious as the revised flight time approached. Suddenly she whispered in his ear, "Hey, have you noticed that old lady over there?" She nodded slightly towards the other side of the lounge. "I thought she was looking at us a while back."

John turned his head slightly. He knew who Deborah meant straight away, as there was only one other person even remotely near. He looked at the old woman for a second or two. She didn't seem interested in them, and was much too far away to hear them.

He tried to reassure her. "Don't worry, we'll be in Oz soon. When we get off the plane and go through Customs, we're ready for our new lives. Nobody will know who we were in England. Nobody will care anyway. They're not prejudiced like the British. The Australians are only interested in who you are and how much you've got, not what's happened in your past life."

"Yeah, still, I can't wait to actually get my feet on Australian soil." She giggled.

"There'll be nothing to connect us with a few killings except our consciences," John reassured her.

She giggled again, "Is that all?"

The flight had not been delayed further, and the journey had not been as tedious as they had expected. John noticed that Deborah's nervousness, slight though it had been, had gone now. She slept reasonably well for part of the flight, although John couldn't. This was not because of any pangs of conscience or worries about some avenging nemesis, but purely because Deborah snored very loudly and kept him awake. He felt relaxed enough though. There was certainly no need for alcohol, which he wanted to avoid in case they overdid it and drew attention to themselves. As he said to Deborah, there would be time enough to relax as soon as they had reached the airport and were away into the hinterland (he was particularly pleased with that word).

Neither of them had ever been to Australia before, although John had a few contacts there, not that he had any intention of calling on any of them. The sooner he and Deborah changed their names and invented new pasts the better.

The landing was gentle, and even Deborah seemed to have enjoyed the flight. That had been what John had been most worried about. He thought that Deborah might have found it too claustrophobic being cooped up in the plane for hours, with the tantalising thought of freedom and comparative wealth at the end of it.

But now they had made it.

It was blisteringly hot as they stepped down onto the airport tarmac. Just as they liked it.

"No roos yet, Deborah," John said, smiling. Seeing a kangaroo in the wild was something Deborah was looking forward to.

In the Customs area, there were quite a few casual but clearly official people standing around. John felt Deborah hesitate momentarily.

"Come on, Deborah, don't let me down now," he said. "They're waiting for some drugs baron or someone like that. You haven't got any Rennies on you, have you?"

She smiled, but it was obviously forced. John was worried whether she would be able to reply innocently if there were any questions. He decided he would have to do all the talking if it became necessary.

Passports were checked, but, as they were moving off, one of the officers stepped forward, "Excuse me, but could you could spare a few moments, please?"

John and Deborah had been stopped before at Customs. Each time they had only had a bottle or two of spirits over the limit, but the officials had never been this deferential before. "Don't worry, Debbie, it's just as it was at Dover that time, remember?" He squeezed her hand: it was clammy, she noticed.

The officers there seemed to know almost everything about them: times, dates, places, who they had killed.

They had both insisted they were innocent, but John knew that Deborah would confess soon enough, and their dreams of an innocent new start in Australia rapidly evaporated.

As they were led from the interview room, they noticed the old lady whom Deborah thought might have been watching them in the airport departure lounge back in Heathrow.

Seeing her waiting there, John's anger flared, and he tried to rush towards her. The officers by his side restrained him.

"So," John blurted out, "Exactly who are you – some detective novelist visiting her relatives in Australia?"

The old lady shrugged. She really did seem so very insignificant.

"I teach deaf children to lip-read," she replied.

Interval

Things were a little quieter in the room now, but it was obvious that tempers were still simmering somewhat, and could erupt again. Professor Guiteras decided there was little he could do, and that it was best to press on with the proceedings.

Henry Dennis was next.

Justice is Done

"Poor old Beakie."

D.C.I. Mullins shook his head sadly.

Any casual listener would have thought he was mourning the demise of his pet budgie. In fact, Henry Mullins was thinking of the life and recent death of Justice Stafford Beak.

Until his murder that morning, Beakie had been presiding over one of those cases that resembles the scenario of a bad Hollywood courtroom drama, complete with witness intimidation and threats to many of those involved in the case. Even Justice Stafford Beak himself had received threatening phone calls.

The Police had taken the threats seriously.

"We decided to put him into a safe house," Henry Mullins continued, "And, as far as I know, no-one with the exception of a few trusted people within the Force has any knowledge of its existence."

"Page-Handley Hall might sound rather grandiose, but it certainly isn't. In fact, it's actually quite small. And it might look ancient, but it isn't really that old. It certainly isn't old enough for a priest hole or hidden rooms, even though we *have* checked. Access to the upper floor from the outside wouldn't be at all easy: there are few pipes, and, anyway, all the walls are white and last night was an extraordinarily bright night."

"I had four men in the garden, all well-hidden, each of them with a good view of one side of the house. Each one had radio contact with the others, and with two mobile units in the surrounding roads."

"Inside, I had two men stationed in the hall, a group in the dining-room, in case someone called for assistance, and even one constable on each side of the bedroom door."

"We'd had to force Beakie to accept a guard. Neither he nor his wife had wanted it, but, after the threats we'd received during the trial, it seemed sensible. Despite the sensational aspects of the case, it wasn't likely to be a long trial, so the Judge and his wife could easily be accommodated in the Hall for a week or so."

"We searched the house each day, and it was guarded even when they weren't there, so no-one could have entered and hidden himself anywhere. There were also no weapons of any sort in the house: we knew exactly what was there and where it was. Despite the guard, all the windows and doors were well-secured, and, although there was a hatch in the ceiling over their bed, there was no-one concealed in the attic, and there was no other access into the roof. Either way, the two windows in the bedroom were nailed and barred."

"And still they got in and killed poor old Beakie."

"His wife woke up at her usual time, and found him dead beside her. Someone had thrust a sharp knife into his heart. She hadn't heard anything, as she'd just been prescribed some sleeping draught, but that's not surprising considering the anxiety she must have been feeling over this business. They both seemed to be trying to keep the traditional stiff upper lip."

"She unlocked the bedroom door, and one of the constables there rushed in (the other correctly remained at his post, and checked that no-one left the room). The Police doctor, Doctor Noyes, was called - Mrs. Beak knew him, as he's the family doctor - and he pronounced that death occurred sometime between three a.m. and the time he was found dead: the usual generous margin for error."

"He was more precise over the murder weapon. He said it was quite long and very thin, and probably professional. He was even able to open his bag and show us almost exactly the sort of knife used. One of the constables asked him to confirm that all his own surgical knives were in place, and that there was nothing missing, which he did. Not that that seemed to be really relevant."

"But we checked Doctor Noyes anyway. His alibi is impeccable, and he doesn't appear to have anything other than a professional interest in the Beak family - well, he definitely isn't having an affair with Mrs. Beak, anyway."

"And it was one of our more intelligent constables that watched Dr. Noyes carefully every second he was in that room. It doesn't pay to trust anybody these days."

"So, short of a conspiracy between almost all of my staff (and we've checked that out as well), the only options seem to be that the Judge committed suicide, which would apparently have been nigh-impossible physically, or that his wife killed him. Apart from the fact that we can find no motive for either, both are impossible as there was no trace of the murder weapon in the room. And there were no such weapons concealed anywhere in the house or attic when we did a most thorough search the afternoon before the murder, and there were none there when we searched the house almost immediately after the murder."

"And there are plenty of people involved in his trial who would be very happy to see his demise."

D.C.I. Mullins was a fairly unsophisticated person, and needed, as he put it, to "get things straightened out in his head."

Even though he had not come anywhere close to solving the crime, he felt he had now gone over the salient points sufficiently and had not left anything important out, so he pulled the flush, and rejoined the rest of his family in the lounge.

He began to think he had perhaps been a little too impassioned in his monologue, judging by the expressions on people's faces.

Back at the Hall later that day, Henry Mullins set in motion the long process of searching everything in the house yet again, this time even more thoroughly.

He was glad he wasn't involved in cancelling and reorganising the trial itself. He had never had any aptitude for that sort of thing, as the lack of a reception at his wedding had proved (as he had pointed out rather indignantly at the time, the wedding cars and the organist *had* been properly booked, even if they had had to ring around for a vicar).

Having outlined everyone's duties and responsibilities, he then sat back and waited for the results of the search, answering any query that arose from his subordinates. When an item was brought to him for instructions as to how to examine it, his usual response was to order it to be broken up into the smallest possible pieces. It was only the presence of the Chief Superintendent, and the shocked expression on his face, that saved a delightful porcelain vase that could patently not have concealed anything larger than a small toenail.

Forensics came up with a disappointing report that was only marginally more precise than the doctor's. Mullins threw it across the floor contemptuously. It came to rest amongst the shards of another vase, less fortunate, but as equally delightful as its twin.

Despite the rigorous search that had taken place, nothing unusual had been unearthed.

Justice Beak had been killed with a long, thin knife, more like one used by a professional than a domestic knife. As no-one, including the doctor, had left without a thorough search, whatever had been used to kill him must still be there. But none of D.C.I. Mullins' staff could find it.

And who had killed him? Someone connected with the court case seemed to be the most likely in terms of a motive, but how had they managed to penetrate the security cordon? Even now, everyone who left the Hall was searched, even himself.

The Judge's wife had the opportunity, after all she was in bed with him, but did she have a motive? And where would she have obtained the weapon? And, more to the point, where had she put the weapon afterwards? The doctor had an unshakeable alibi, but he also had a bag full of knives. However, he had confirmed that they were all accounted for, and Beakie had certainly been dead before his arrival. All the policemen there had been with the Force for many years, and D.C.I. Mullins could vouch for their trustworthiness himself, much as he would have liked to have found some scapegoat.

"Hell," he said out loud, as usual to nobody in particular.

"Any thoughts?" Henry Mullins said, this time to P.C. Crowther. He really just wanted to think aloud, but Crowther was hanging around the office. As Crowther usually made little input to any conversation and what he did say was rarely relevant, Mullins didn't think he would intrude too much on his soliloquy, but in this he was to some extent disappointed.

"Well, I'm a great believer in criminal psychology," Crowther said thoughtfully, his mouth moving slowly and cautiously, as if he were chewing gum, which he wasn't. "I reckon phrenology was a pretty good idea, if only they'd let it develop a little more."

"I also think there's a lot you can learn just from looking at someone's face. I took the chance to have a good look at both Mrs. Beak and Doctor Noyes that morning. She seemed a little agitated, as you'd expect, but he looked about as calm as at the surgery. If either of them had been the murderer, I'm sure I would have detected some facial evidence straight away."

"My main worry is how the murder weapon vanished," the Constable continued.

"I happen to have read quite a few detective novels myself ..." (here we go, thought Mullins) "... and I'm convinced it was either made of something, er, biodegradable, er, like ice, or something that could be ground down as it were, and made almost invisible, like glass."

"No, no, no," D.C.I. Mullins shook his head, "I'm sure the Forensic people would have found something in either case. They do know what to look for, I can assure you."

"Well, then," Crowther chewed on, "Someone must have got down that chimney, then."

The D.C.I. shook his head again, "No, it was too narrow, and it was sealed with bars, anyway."

P.C. Crowther, known for some reason to his colleagues as Wrigley, had a final try, "A monkey, perhaps?"

It was as young Darren Mullins was hammering on the toilet door enquiring after his father's health that Henry Mullins had a thought. Thinking hard had always been rather a strain for him.

His ideas usually started as a niggling worry, and then grew into a more complex theory over a period of a few weeks, as he worked at them and pruned them, rather as if they were an elegant piece of topiary. This time, however, his superior officers were pressing him for swift action, and all they were likely to get from Henry Mullins in the short period of time available was a badly hacked piece of privet.

It would have been better if he hadn't wasted time listening to that young fool Crowther, he thought.

But there was something odd he had said.

When would he ever have seen Doctor Noyes in his surgery? Was he Crowther's doctor as well?

He phoned him up straight away on his mobile.

"You said Doctor Noyes was as calm as at his surgery. Is he your doctor too?" Mullins asked. Even on the phone he could hear Crowther chewing as he thought.

"No, but we had to call into the Doctor's place on the way to collect Justice Beak from the Court the day before the murder," Crowther replied ruminatively. "Mrs. Beak asked me to collect her from the Hall first, as she wanted to visit the surgery to collect some prescription. I naturally stayed with her."

Mullins needed to think. He blotted out the noise of the hammering on the door, and pondered deeply.

"So how did you work it all out?" Henry Mullins' boss enquired.

"Well, we knew there were no weapons in the house before the judge and his wife arrived. We know there were none after the Doctor left. We know the Doctor had his full complement of medical knives when he left. So the only conclusion was that he didn't have the full set when he arrived."

"And that was because Mrs. Beak had taken one out of his bag when she had visited him the day before. She counted on his not needing to check very often to see if one were missing. As soon as he arrived, she put it back in his bag."

"In fact, she relied on our not suspecting the truth so much that we had no difficulty in finding plenty of evidence all over the murder weapon." He beamed happily.

"And what was her motive then?"

D.C.I. Henry Mullins' expression changed slightly. He always felt less confident when considering what he referred to as "non-tangibles." The thing to do was to catch the murderer, and then find the motive. Dig deeply enough, and you'll always find something.

In fact, as she would later confess, Mrs. Beak had been upset because of her husband's secret romantic liaison with a much younger lady, an aspiring actress no less, and the possibility of an impending divorce. The turbulent case over which Justice Stafford Beak was presiding provided a suitable alternative motive that his wife had hoped would prevent anyone enquiring too closely into her own marital situation.

Henry Mullins regained his composure.

"Well, you know what woman are like, Sir," he said, and winked broadly.

Interval

Penny Jones was beginning to fidget.

Noticeably so.

The Professor decided to call her to the front of the room for her story before her nervousness reached even greater proportions.

Upstairs and Downstairs, and in My Lady's Chamber

The desk sergeant at Upper Wormham Police Station was enjoying one of the many quiet periods during his working day, his mind deep in thought about the forthcoming rugby match against Ballchester Police R.F.C., whilst his fingers deftly extracted the contents of his left ear using the cap of a biro.

The telephone rang. The desk sergeant examined the biro cap thoughtfully for a few seconds before answering the call.

He started to say "Upper Wormham Police Station here. How can I help you?" but was interrupted by the caller.

"You'd better come at once," a voice whispered down the phone, "Lady Pooley has been murdered."

The desk sergeant immediately recognised the voice of Mrs. Burke (no-one knew if she had a first name), who was Lady Pooley's housekeeper at Branham Hall. Even though she was speaking very quietly, as she habitually did, she still managed to convey her alarm and shock at the situation. The desk sergeant neglected to say his usual, "Hold on a minute while I write all this down, Madam," and instead said, "I'll get the Inspector to the Hall right away."

"You'd better bring some hefty constables too," Mrs. Burke added, "She's locked in her room, and the door's solid oak."

"Why does it have to happen when I'm on duty?" Inspector Jeffcott thought.

Luckily, all the constables available were well-built. Constables Bright and Williams in particular would be perfect for battering down doors, as they were in the Station's Rugby Team. P.C. Burns, also pretty sturdy, volunteered to come along as well. The four of them crammed themselves into a Ford Escort, and set off for Branham Hall, two miles away from the village.

There was a long twisting driveway up to the house. It had probably been landscaped at one time so that each turn of the drive would reveal a new view of the house before finally opening out to show the house in all its splendour, but most of the trees had been felled recently, so that the effect had been rather diminished.

In truth, Branham Hall was a rather nasty building. Each of its facades was rather bleak, consisting of plain and unadorned windows set in a wall of unrelieved grey stonework. The only frivolity in its architecture was the plethora of assorted and totally asymmetric chimneys, spires, and cupolas on the roof, which made the whole house resemble a large grey box in a children's nursery, with all the toys sticking untidily out of the top.

The house's only real redemption was its entrance, which was rather imposing, consisting of a grand Palladian portico behind a large and impressive set of steps. Mindful of the urgency of the situation, Inspector Jeffcott brought the Escort to a stop with the front offside wheel on the bottom step.

Mrs. Burke was waiting for them in front of the main door. She appeared to have recovered to some extent, as her "This way, Inspector" seemed more suited to her inviting someone in for tea and cucumber sandwiches than to view a dead body.

The policemen were led into the main foyer, a huge hallway at the far end of which an immense staircase led up to the first floor. Although the Inspector had visited Branham Hall a couple of times before, each time on business, he had never had occasion to visit the upper floor, and so had to rely on Mrs. Burke to show them the way up the grand staircase, rather asthmatically it has to be said.

Lady Pooley's suite overlooked both the East side and the front drive. Mrs. Burke indicated the door to her Ladyship's suite. Inspector Jeffcott rushed ahead and tried the handle. As he had been told to expect, it was locked.

"Why do you think Lady Pooley's dead?" he asked.

Mrs. Burke indicated a sideboard, "I climbed onto that to look through the small window over the door." Inspector Jeffcott also clambered onto the sideboard, from where there was a clear view into the room beyond. Her Ladyship herself lay slumped over her escritoire, a knife clearly visible in her back. She was obviously dead.

She was also obviously murdered.

Inspector Jeffcott tried the door again, this time more forcibly, but it was solidly locked, and he realised the sturdy oak door would require a lot of force to break it open. "O.K. Bright, Williams, the door, if you please," he said, realising he sounded as if he merely wanted it opened for him.

The two stars of Upper Wormham Police R.F.C. charged at the door six times before the lock finally gave way, and the door burst open. The policemen stood still for a moment to take in the scene, which was exactly as the Inspector had seen through the little window.

Lady Pooley lay over her writing desk. The knife in her back appeared to be a letter-opener. The room looked very neat and orderly, but rather impersonal. There were two windows, both locked from the inside. Through a door to the right, her Ladyship's bedroom was visible, its windows, also found to be locked from the inside, overlooking the front drive.

Inspector Jeffcott went with P.C. Bright to examine the body. P.C. Williams investigated the room in case anyone were hidden, but this room was simply-furnished and would give little chance for concealment. He went to join P.C. Burns searching the bedroom. Here, there were more places in which one might hide, but they could find nothing of consequence here either. There was definitely nobody concealed in the two rooms.

"What's galling me," said Inspector Jeffcott in the bar of his local, 'The Rose and Anchor,' "Is how anyone could have stabbed Lady Pooley. If I can't find out how, then I'll have to put it down as suicide, but, according to the medical evidence, that seems unlikely, if not downright impossible."

"Forensics and the technical departments have been all over that suite now. The only door out of the suite was definitely securely locked on the inside, and nobody could have fiddled *that* lock. Nobody could have locked it from the outside using wires or whatever, either. The same applies to the windows. There were no trap-doors, no hidden recesses, no priest holes, nothing like that. So, in short, there is absolutely no way anyone could have left those rooms, and nowhere anyone could have stayed hidden."

"And Lady Pooley couldn't have generously locked the door after her murderer had left, as death would have been more or less instantaneous," he added.

Inspector Jeffcott was talking to his ex-colleague Herbert Wright, now retired. He had already gone over the most salient details of his recent visit to Branham Hall, and was now hoping someone, most likely someone else, would have a flash of inspiration.

Herbert Wright sat deep in thought for a minute or two, clearly wrestling with some difficult mental problem. After a while, his face brightened. "It's definitely your round, Jeff," he said.

Inspector Jeffcott ignored this statement, as he usually did.

"So what do you think, Herbert?" he asked.

"I don't know," Herbert Wright shifted in his seat. "However, I do wonder why Mrs. Burke took you all up that grand staircase."

"Er, why should that have any bearing on the case?"

Herbert Wright continued, "Did you examine the layout of Branham Hall?"

Inspector Jeffcott shook his head.

"I wouldn't have thought the servants would have been allowed to use such a palatial staircase, so there must be some other way of getting to the first floor. As the staircase was at the back of the hall, I was wondering whether there mightn't be a more modest set of stairs, perhaps hidden behind what looks like a cupboard door, towards the front of the building, allowing servants access to the upper floor, and to her Ladyship's suite. In fact, there must be."

"And, *if there were*, I would have thought that Mrs. Burke would have taken you upstairs that way. I mean, I know that the Police are still fairly respected ... well, around here at least ... and I'm not suggesting that you should have been made to use the tradesman's entrance, but, given the gravity of the situation, the quickest and most direct way of reaching her Ladyship's suite would have been the most sensible."

It was the Inspector's turn to shift in his seat, "Yes, I'm sure you're right. But, even if you are, that still doesn't solve our little crime."

"It might do if you can remember exactly what happened that day. You say Bright and Williams smashed down the door, and then you all rushed in to examine the body."

"Well, Bright and myself examined the body. Williams went to check the room to see if anyone were hidden, and Burns checked the bedroom."

"Are you sure?" Herbert enquired.

"Well, yes. Where else would we all have been?"

"Well, if Burns could have taken this quicker route to her Ladyship's suite, he could have entered through the *unlocked* door, and then locked the door and waited in the bedroom for you to smash your way in. In the confusion, no-one would have realised that they hadn't actually seen him entering Lady Pooley's suite."

The Inspector was worried. "But why? Mrs. Burke said that she had seen Lady Pooley with a knife in her back, and that the door was locked, when she telephoned the Station."

"Then I reckon it must have been Mrs. Burke who killed Lady Pooley. It was probably done on the spur of the moment and the rest of the plan worked out quickly afterwards. Mrs. Burke could have phoned P.C. Burns at the police station to explain the situation before she telephoned you."

"Of course, it's possible that Mrs. Burke only *said* that her Ladyship had been stabbed, and then waited for P.C. Burns to arrive and actually do the deed, but that seems less likely doesn't it?"

Inspector Jeffcott looked unsure.

"All this wouldn't give P.C. Burns very much time, but it would probably be enough."

Inspector Jeffcott looked unsure a little more.

Herbert Wright sat wriggling in his seat for a few seconds. "Is P.C. Burns related to Mrs. Burke, by any chance?"

Inspector Jeffcott's face brightened up, "No, he isn't ... but he will be when he marries her daughter in a few months' time!"

"So, if his prospective mother-in-law were to kill her Ladyship … she might say it was an accident … P.C. Burns *might* be induced to cover it up, eh?"

"Maybe." Inspector Jeffcott accepted, "He hasn't been in the Force that long. But why should Mrs. Burke murder her employer?"

"There could be a number of reasons. I gather there are often disagreements between servants and their masters or mistresses. I would have thought a premeditated crime rather unlikely."

Herbert Wright had an afterthought, "I don't suppose Mrs. Burke or her daughter were short of money and she was likely to inherit ..."

"I don't know. I'll get someone to look into that first thing in the morning." Inspector Jeffcott stared into his empty glass, "I'll have to check the layout of Branham Hall, but I'm sure that that was how it was done. Maybe we should interview Burke and Burns separately, to check that their stories agree."

"I'll just have to grill 'em 'til they crack."

Herbert Wright was less surprised by this lapse in Inspector Jeffcott's linguistic style than by his subsequent offer to buy the next round.

Interval

Roger Atkinson had originally rather hoped that things would have been dealt with alphabetically.

However, as he was in one of Professor Guiteras' classes, he should have known how little he cared for any sort of order.

The Professor's eyes roamed the room looking for those he had not yet selected. He had to look particularly hard to locate some who were deliberately hiding themselves behind others.

Roger was one of these.

He looked out cautiously to see at whom the Professor was looking, but his timing was inopportune. Their eyes met.

He was summoned.

Casualty of War

Chief Inspector Charlie Mugford had always been a passenger on his holidays.

His wife had always organised not only the reservation, but also every tiny detail of each day. And that had suited Charlie Mugford perfectly.

But now, for the first time in his life, he was taking a holiday on his own. His dear wife had passed away six months earlier, and it was only now that he felt he could face up to travelling on his own. He also realised that he needed a break, both away from his job and from his home.

Therefore, he had decided to book two weeks' holiday at a hotel near to where he had spent his childhood, at Nether Bottom.

Even though he had not had to book any transport, he was still surprised how easy it had been to make the reservation. Just one telephone call had been enough to book the room. As he was a Chief Inspector, they even trusted him enough not to ask for a deposit.

But, if booking the holiday had been easy, finding things with which to occupy himself whilst he was there was not so easy. He had armed himself with a plethora of shiny leaflets from the foyer of the hotel, but, after just two days, he had visited all the places of interest that he felt might have been.

It was on the first Tuesday of his holiday that he realised that what he really wanted was some Police work to do.

He relished the thought of at least some petty crime to investigate, or at best some glorious murder.

He enquired eagerly at the hotel bar that evening as to whether any unsolved felonies had been committed in the area recently.

The landlord smiled happily. "Now, don't you go worrying about that, Sir. I can assure you that Nether Bottom is as safe as houses. There's no crime here at all. Nothing untoward ever happens here."

Charlie Mugford thought to himself that it looked as if nothing at all ever happened here. He said something to that effect and bemoaned the lack of crime in the area.

The Landlord became rather solicitous, and leant forwards across the bar. "Now, if you're looking for some wrongdoing, you'd be better off in Eddington, that's our nearest big city. You'd like it there, Sir: they've got an awful lot of crime. But that's fifty miles away, so that's not much use to you."

"To tell you the truth, Sir, we haven't had any crimes here for, well, since as far back as I can remember." The landlord raised his hands from the bar apologetically, and moved off to serve a customer who was growing rather impatient.

Charlie Mugford felt very inclined to pack his bags and leave out of sheer boredom. As the landlord looked exceedingly old, as far back as he could remember was likely to be at least fifty years or so. The Chief Inspector hoped he were an amnesiac.

This situation often seemed to arise in detective books or television thrillers, but the outcome was always far more interesting. The final scene would be the headline in some local newspaper, 'The Nether Bottom Rag' perhaps, "Chief Inspector Mugford Brilliantly Solves Fifty-Year-Old Murder."

But things never happened like that in real life.

He decided to give it one more day.

There were one or two things of minor interest in the immediate vicinity of Nether Bottom, both of which he had already visited, but there seemed hardly anything at all within the village itself. Fond memories of places played in or partially demolished by Little Spotty Mugford were dissipated by the fact that he hardly recognised anything at all in the village. It was clear that the village had become a dormitory town for Eddington, even at fifty miles distant, and any beautiful old buildings had now been replaced by ugly, but more up-to-date habitations.

But there was still the old statue in the square. As a boy, he had never read the inscription, but he now thought that it was about time that he did.

The statue looked like any other statue erected by a grateful village to its dead in one or both World Wars. It showed a heavily-bearded infantryman, apparently injured or fatigued or both, struggling to hold a large flag. But this statue was not placed atop a plaque listing all those who had fought for the freedom of future generations: instead, there was only one name carved onto the plinth. In large letters was written "Our Bill." Below, in much smaller letters as if further explanation were not really necessary, "William Mitchell 1894-1918." The sculptor must have felt that this was enough, for there were no descriptions of his deeds or the battles at which he had fought. The little grass patch in front of the statue was well tended, and the whole statue seemed looked after. Even the village pigeons seemed to have respected it.

"Who was Old Bill?" asked the Chief Inspector back in the hotel bar that evening.

"*Our* Bill," the landlord replied, "Was Nether Bottom's greatest hero. He fought gallantly and conspicuously in all the great battles of the First World War." He sounded as if he were reading from a guide book.

"We know all about his bravery and heroism because one of the local reporters on the 'Nether Bottom and District Times' (the paper's gone now, of course) found out about him, and adopted him, I suppose you could say. Bill Mitchell's mother lived just behind the Church (lovely carvings aren't they?). My father knew the family fairly well, and said Bill was always so modest and unassuming, so we probably would never have heard about him if Paul Wheeler hadn't decided that the world should hear of his exploits. I've read some of his articles. Some people said he was really quite an average reporter, but his war reports were truly outstanding. Well, I don't suppose any writer could have gone wrong with stirring tales about Our Bill. His articles were so good that they were taken up by one of the big London papers. After a year or two, Paul moved up to London, to Fleet Street, to write, but London life couldn't have suited him. A few years after the War, he came back to work here again."

"I've read most of the articles. You can too if you want, Sir. Most of them are in our local Museum by the Church. I thought some of them must have been exaggerated, but, years ago, I was able to check with the local boys who'd fought in the Somme and elsewhere, and all of them had seen Bill in some battle or other, and they all confirmed the stories. He was a hell of a man, Our Bill."

The Museum turned out to be the curator's front parlour. It was very small, but it seemed adequate for the number of exhibits on show (in fact, truth to be told, even the small parlour was only sparsely stocked). The Curator, Lionel Bland, personally conducted all visitors around the Museum, perhaps because he wanted to check that they didn't venture into his lounge as well.

Chief Inspector Mugford asked about the newspapers from the First World War. He didn't really need to ask, as their display was in the centre of the room, but he felt that he couldn't just walk up and start reading them, in the same way that he couldn't have done so in the front room of anyone else's house.

He found the newspapers engrossing. As he was clearly a respectable fellow, Curator Bland left him alone with the exhibits after ten minutes, and went to attend to his boiled ham.

The stories were as the landlord had said. Written in a surprisingly vivid style, they painted what seemed a very real and accurate image of what the War must have been like. Life in the trenches was described in all its muddy squalor, making the glorious heroism of our men all the more rousing. All the British forces were praised, especially the local men who were often referred to personally, but one name was repeated more frequently than any other, and, after a few months, the articles began to concern themselves almost exclusively with this soldier. The name William Mitchell was used for few weeks, but very soon his full name was dropped, and thereafter only Our Bill was mentioned.

Paul Wheeler had even been posted out to France for first-hand reports. That must have been an ambitious venture for such a small newspaper as the 'N B & D T,' but it was obvious that, by that stage, interest in the local hero had become national, and the stories were even being copied to many other newspapers.

One of the last articles had been written almost fifty years previously, in 1918.

"MYSTERY SURROUNDING OUR HERO" was the headline.

"Where is Our Bill?" was below this in slightly smaller print, whilst "Our Gallant Boys Return from the Front" was in even smaller print below that.

"It was a cold, depressing afternoon that found me waiting on Nether Bottom Station platform," wrote Paul Wheeler. "The train pulled in, and, weary and tired, our Boys stepped onto the platform to be greeted by their families and the village dignitaries. But where was our Hero? That he had been on the train was certain: I later talked with some of the soldiers who had travelled down on the train, and found out that he had indeed been on the train with them when it left London. Some of them were proud that he had played cards with them for some of the journey, before he had retired to "compose himself" just after Jervay's Fen Station, the last station before Nether Bottom. But he certainly did not alight at Nether Bottom. He did not remain on board: when Our Bill could not be found, all the carriages were scrupulously checked. And he certainly did not leave the train by the other side, as some workmen were able to testify. It is gratifying to have our Boys back with those who love them, but we cannot be content until we know the fate of Our Bill."

Paul Wheeler's last article in the museum was dated the next day. "MYSTERY SOLVED" the headline ran, before repeating the details from the previous day's news, although it is doubtful if any of the villagers would not have already read it.

"I asked some soldiers, the very ones who had enjoyed a game of cards with the Great Man, what they thought had happened. It appears that Our Bill was not in the same jubilant mood as his fellow fighters. He felt he had served his country well, and had proved himself in battle, but could not imagine himself returning to a normal life again. He was pleased that the War was indeed over, and did not wish that any more gallant lads should die, but he did not feel that there was a place for him in peacetime again. Only God knows what our Hero must have endured in the name of Justice and Peace, and it is possible that his mind may have been tortured by what he had seen. His final words were that he had to compose himself, as he expected there would be a great many people to greet them at the station. After four years of War and Bloodshed, he made it clear that he did not relish the idea of again becoming part of Society, a Society that could create a War such as he had been through."

"After Jervay's Fen Station, the line crosses a vast tract of marshland. There are places below the railway where a man might land, and sink, and never be found. It is my contention that, as William Mitchell took leave of his friends at this point, he jumped, or perhaps allowed himself to fall, from the train into this marsh."

"That such a good man should feel that he could no longer enjoy our peaceful society after his dreadful experiences is a dire comment on the whole sin of War."

Paul Wheeler finished, "If we hear no more of this Man, then we can feel perhaps grateful to some extent that he is now at Peace from the horrors of War. We should strive in his name to ensure that no man again has to endure such torture and pain."

The curator had mainly used Paul Wheeler's articles from the local paper to bring to life Our Bill's story. There were a few copies on display of the national broadsheets that had also reprinted the stories, but these were clearly only there to indicate how important Our Bill was to the whole nation, not just to Nether Bottom. However, one of the broadsheets at the end of the section was written by another reporter, and seemed intended to complete the story of Our Bill's last journey from the London end.

"I mingled with the crowds at the Station," an Arthur Blunt wrote. "It was strange to see our gallant lads just as we have always remembered them, but yet so different, burdened as they were with the aromas and smells of a war in a foreign land. Glad to be back on English soil once again, they began to relax, although it will be some time before they can believe that the horrors they have seen are no longer reality, and are over, hopefully for ever. I decided to journey with them back to Wiltshire, not to harass them or ask them to talk to me for the Paper, but merely to listen to their tales and stories, and to absorb the joyful atmosphere. Our Bill, himself a Wiltshire lad, was ensconced in a corner, playing cards with a group of soldiers, men that he had probably never encountered beforehand, but now great pals. He seemed to be losing each hand, but not caring. To lose at something so trivial perhaps seemed so very unimportant to him. In fact, his good humour filled and cheered a train that was full of tired and exhausted men. After a small station in the marshes, he left the card players and took a stroll in my direction. I had no wish to bother this fine gentleman, but asked only for a few words. He seemed happy to oblige, and spoke with me for quite a few minutes. Although only twenty-four years of age, he seemed inordinately wise and philosophical. Then he passed along the carriage, away from me, and I never saw him again. The person most responsible for bringing the daring exploits of Our Bill to our attention, local reporter Paul Wheeler, looked upset that he had not been able to have an interview with him just before arriving at Nether Bottom Station, and perhaps he even intended joining him in a grand entrance into the village. But in this he was disappointed. When the locomotive lumbered into Nether Bottom Station, Our Bill was no longer on board."

Charlie Mugford felt the article hinted at some refined professional rivalry or even jealousy. He thanked the curator, who was just starting his lunch, and went for a long walk beside a disused canal. Kicking cans was still as much fun as he remembered it was.

The landlord of the hotel confessed himself pleased that the Chief Inspector had found enough to keep himself interested.

"Folks don't seem so interested in things like that these days. If you find it interesting, though, you ought to talk to old Wheeler."

Charlie Mugford's face contorted as he did some mental calculations. "Let's see, it's 1967 now, and he must have been at least twenty in 1918, so he must be around seventy now."

"Mmm, he lives over by the Church, Barkus' Cottage. Horrible little terraced hovel. Nasty bit of architecture that," the landlord muttered.

A short, grubby, and seemingly ancient man opened the door.

"Good afternoon. I am Chief Inspector Mugford. I have reason to believe that you may be able to assist us in our enquiries into the death of William Mitchell." Well, that is what he would have liked to have said. What he actually said was, "Good afternoon. I have been reading and enjoying your interesting articles about Our Bill in the Museum."

"You'd want me Dad," the creature said, before calling for him, and then vanishing back into the dark recesses of the terraced house.

"Dad" looked much younger than his son, and received the repeated salutation gratefully and with obvious pleasure. "Won't you come in, please?" he asked.

They spent almost an hour discussing the articles of wartime heroics and the author's rather less successful subsequent career with a "quality newspaper" in London. Chief Inspector Mugford felt it was time to try and clarify a few things that worried him.

"So where did Our Bill die? Was it at Ypres?" he enquired.

"No, no, didn't you read the final articles?" Paul Wheeler remonstrated. "He vanished off the train that was bringing him and the other lads back to Nether Bottom."

Charlie Mugford looked thoughtful. "Reading through your articles, I have to say that I felt, especially towards the end of the War, that the stories about Our Bill were becoming more and more, shall we say, unlikely, but I put most of it down to artistic licence and patriotic exaggeration, and …"

Paul Wheeler interrupted, "Come on, this was in the middle of the War, you know. I felt bad enough being rejected for active service. The least I could do to contribute was to try to cheer up the nation with some stirring propaganda. That's normal for the Press during times of war, you know." He smiled as if he were talking to a small child.

"But your final few articles about Our Bill's supposed death were just too romantic to be true. It might have sounded good, but it was more like a cheap novel than a series of newspaper articles. Things just don't happen like that in real life. You can manipulate the facts about someone's life, and lie and exaggerate about his deeds as much as you like, but you shouldn't fake someone's death."

"Are you suggesting that I murdered him?" Wheeler said, with a look in his eye that was more amused than outraged.

"Oh no. No. Not exactly," Charlie Mugford said quickly. "Reading through the articles, I began to get some idea of the truth, but what finally convinced me was the article in the Museum that was written by Arthur Blunt. It must have been quite a scoop for him, being able to report on Our Bill's triumphant return on the train, and even to interview him. And all this time you were waiting patiently at the station here in Nether Bottom. Bearing in mind that you had chronicled Our Bill's exploits for more than two years, I would have thought your Editor would have insisted on your accompanying Our Bill on the train home, especially since they had earlier managed to find the money to send you to the Somme. The scoop must have surprised our Mr. Blunt, too. Especially since, if his reporting was accurate, he actually saw you there on the train that day … but that, of course, was after you had …"

"… Slit his throat and thrown him off the train into the mire?" Paul Wheeler asked, a youthfully impish expression appearing on his lined face.

"No, no, no," insisted Charlie Mugford, "I thought at first that he might never have existed at all, but he was clearly once an inhabitant of the village, and his family lived around here. But William Mitchell died fairly early on in the War, didn't he?" Charlie Mugford asked, before guessing, "He wasn't really much of a soldier, was he?"

"Undistinguished is the word I would have used," Wheeler nodded, a faraway expression coming into his eyes. "I did ask Lionel to remove Blunt's article from his Museum, but he never throws anything away."

The Chief Inspector continued, "But why did you chose William Mitchell? Did you know him?"

Paul Wheeler shook his head. "Not really. I'd probably seen him around the village …"

"But you decided to create a legend around him. Perhaps, when you were sent over to report on the War, you were with him when he died, and you were able to convince the officers of the merits of your morale-boosting plan. Perhaps you were able to intercept the official telegram. But somehow you must have stopped the notice of his death arriving. I suppose it was better for all concerned that he should be thought of as a hero. The lads fighting had someone to live up to, and to die for. Morale here and throughout the country was boosted. And old Mrs Mitchell believed she had a hero for a son"

"And all the other soldiers backed up your stories, because everyone wanted to have met Our Bill and to have fought with him, to share his glory, and to die for him."

"But what do you do when peace arrives, and everyone awaits Our Bill's return? That must have been a bit of a shock for you, Mr. Wheeler. So you dress up to match your description of Our Bill, and you join the train in London. After acting conspicuously throughout most of the journey, you change back into yourself just prior to Nether Bottom Station."

Paul Wheeler smiled. "Actually, I'm rather relieved that someone finally knows the truth. I wouldn't have liked it to have got about before his mother's death, but she passed away a number of years ago. She was still a celebrity right up to her death."

"So (Chief Inspector, was it?), are you going to arrest me for William Mitchell's murder?" Paul Wheeler asked.

"I think it's just a little too late now," Charlie Mugford said, smiling.

Then he suddenly thought of something.

"But you were a newspaperman. You don't know of any unsolved murders in the area, do you?"

Interval

Heather Davies stood up impatiently.

"Look, it's very late, and my mother's probably worried. I *have* to go."

Professor Guiteras put on a passable Vincent Price voice.

He held up what looked like a front door key.

"Sorry, my dear, but the front door is locked, and you haven't *paid* for your evening. What a spread! What wines!"

"I *demand* my story."

He didn't fool anybody ... except Heather.

Sheepishly she shuffled up to the rostrum and started to speak hesitantly.

Truck Stop

Joseph was the apple of Felicity Aston-Pendlebury's eye. Felicity herself was very thin and willowy, with the exception of her shoulders, which were exceptionally broad, and a rapidly-developing set of biceps. Her blonde hair was cropped, perhaps excessively close, and she never wore make-up. Joseph was the name with which she had christened her two-year-old Volvo tractor unit. Even she didn't know why.

It was unfortunate that she had decided to drive her lorry through Oughton Oggleby that Friday, July the ninth, at three in the afternoon. The only route from the nearby industrial estate to the M4 passed right through the middle of the village, and campaigners had been lobbying for a bypass for many years without success.

Having just negotiated the tight turn by the seventeenth-century market hall (leaving it still standing intact, unlike some lorry-drivers), she was driving out of the village, when, from between the last two buildings on the left, something shot out right in front of her. She braked sharply, and clouds of dust from the dry road rose into the village air. Her reactions were quick, but not quick enough.

Lying in the road behind the trailer was the body, clearly deceased, of an elderly gentleman around seventy-five. He was dressed in what seemed to her to be his gardening clothes, although perhaps those were what he habitually wore at home. Felicity noticed he seemed to be smiling.

Within a few seconds, she was joined by a man who had been standing over the road and who must have witnessed it all ("Thank God," thought Felicity), and an elderly lady holding a small spade.

Felicity quickly looked around to get her bearings. It wasn't the first accident she had been involved in, although it was the first that had resulted in an injury, let alone a fatality, and she automatically checked the layout of the road and the buildings in preparation for the various forms she would have to fill in later. She would take some photographs when it was quieter.

The two buildings seemed to consist of an old farmhouse with, adjacent to it on the side away from the village, a larger farm building. There appeared to be no actual farm nearby, so perhaps the farm building was now disused, or was used as a garage or for general storage. Both buildings were built right up to the edge of the road, with no pavement at that point.

Between the two buildings was the opening from which the elderly gentleman had appeared. It was a narrow sloping alley, just wide enough for pedestrians, cycles, and suchlike. It no doubt gave access to the entrance to the farmhouse at the rear, as no doors were visible on the side nearest the road. An aid to visibility was provided by a modern and rather domestic-looking mirror propped up amongst some ivy fairly high up on the wall of the opening. However, the entrance to this alley was now partially blocked off by a low wall, about ten inches high, so that only pedestrians could easily use it.

Thoughts of pedestrians brought Felicity's mind back to what had happened, and the need to do something. Simultaneously, it seemed, the elderly lady became more aware of the situation too, and said to her, "I'd better stay here with him. Do you think you could go inside the house and telephone for an ambulance ... and the Police as well, I suppose? The telephone's just on the right as you go inside the door."

"There's no need," replied Felicity, "I have a phone in the cab." She hopped up (once quite a feat for her, but now merely a single quick movement), reached inside for the handset, and made the call.

As though only now realising what had happened, the elderly lady began to look more than a little upset.

Detective Wing was the first policeman to arrive on the scene. He took Felicity's statement first, to allow time for the other two, who were more elderly, to adjust to the situation. Then he turned to the elderly lady, a Mrs. Smith, who it turned out was the wife of the man who had been killed.

Detective Wing frequently had to talk to the elderly, and felt he knew how to communicate with them both effectively and sympathetically. However, this talent consisted mainly of shouting at them in case they were hard-of-hearing (he used the same approach with those who couldn't understand English). Mrs. Smith was looking away from him at the time he finished talking to Felicity (she appeared to be tending the flowers in a small window-box), but totally failed to respond to even the loudest of Detective Wing's enquiries.

The witness who had been standing over the road, Mr. Standish, butted in, "She's profoundly deaf, I'm afraid." He made vague circular motions with his right hand near to his ear. "She can lip-read pretty well, but she can't hear you at all when she's facing away from you."

Detective Wing decided to leave his interview with Mrs. Smith until after he had talked to Mr. Standish. He began his account enthusiastically as soon as he was prompted, "Well, I was walking back from the fields with my dog, Chaucer, when I saw this lorry approaching." Detective Wing looked around him, unable to find any dog. "Oh no, no, he will have run home by now. He doesn't like any unpleasantness."

"Anyway, I had just got to the old Mill Land there," he pointed vaguely across the road, "When I saw this heavy goods vehicle approaching. Not that there's anything unusual in that! I'd like to say that it was speeding, but I'm afraid it was actually going very slowly and carefully. Anyway, poor Mr. Smith shot out from that little alley of his at a fair lick right under its wheels. He must have tripped on that low wall, poor man. Well, when we got to him, there wasn't anything anyone could do."

"The lorry must have been travelling at less than twenty miles per hour, I suppose. I know a little bit about lorries and speeds, because I've been on the Bypass Committee with Mr. and Mrs. Smith for quite a few years. Well, Mr. Smith likes to get involved on the periphery as it were. Not that our campaigning has met with much success. Despite the, you know ..." (Mr. Standish pointed to one of his ears), "... Mrs. Smith has been one of the most active and prominent members of the Committee."

"Did you see anybody else around?" asked the detective.

Mr. Standish said that he hadn't.

Detective Wing turned to Mrs. Smith, and put himself between her and the window-box.

"Do you feel you are able to talk to us yet, Mrs. Smith?" Detective Wing said. "I'm sure you must be deeply distressed."

"No, no, there's nothing that a little judicious weeding can't cure," she replied, poking around in the window-box. Detective Wing wondered whether she had heard him correctly, and then decided that she had.

"I was in the kitchen, shelling peas, when I heard this dreadful squeal of brakes. It was quite, quite dreadful. I thought straight away 'That's Arthur," but it wasn't. It was my husband." Arthur happily snuffled around in the gutter.

"He looked so serene lying there. He must have gone out to put something in the dustbin, some circulars I expect, lost his balance, tripped or whatever - it's a bit uneven there and there's a low wall - and fallen into the road."

By now, the ambulance had come and gone, but Mrs. Smith clearly felt she should wait there in case she were required again. She got out a small fork from her apron and began to attack the window-box more vigorously.

By now, Detective Wing's colleague, Watson, had appeared. The two policemen walked up the short alley. The floor consisted of rough-hewn stones, upon which someone might indeed lose his or her footing and trip. It might become quite slippery and dangerous when it rained, but there had been no rain for several days and it was dry and dusty. There was a plastic dustbin near the road, but this must have recently been emptied, as there were only a few papers in it. The alley sloped upwards from the road, and opened onto a large lawned and wooded area at the back. The only door to the house was here at the rear, to the left. To the right lay the old farm building. It was obviously largely disused, and a wooden ladder, a small hand cart, and a plethora of old rusty tools and farm machinery lay just inside the half-rotten door. There was an open stone stairway outside, presumably leading up to a loft above the farm building.

Further investigations yielded nothing more of any interest, so the two police officers took their leave of Mrs. Smith, and, the road having now been cleared, retired to their cars over the road.

On Wing's suggestion, they both drove off, parked one car in front of the church, and quickly returned in Watson's car to a small road opposite the farmhouse. From this vantage point they had a good view of it. The car was fitted with a video recording camera, which they turned on.

"The way I see it," said Detective Wing, "Is that it *could* have been an accident. Against that is that Mr. Smith, according to two witnesses, apparently careered out of that alley at some speed, more than I can imagine he could have attained with his own physical abilities and natural gravitational forces. Also, it seems rather a coincidence that he should arrive in front of the lorry with such perfect timing. There isn't that much traffic on this road at all. As you will have noticed, there have hardly been any vehicles passing during the hour or so that we've been here. I accept that most of what there is consists of heavy goods vehicles though, and these roads *are* inadequate for that. I can understand the local people worrying."

"If Mr. Smith had fallen onto the road a few seconds earlier, Miss Felicity whatnot, being young and alert, would probably have been able to stop at that speed, or at least swerved. Had he fallen a few seconds later, landing in the road after the lorry had passed, he would only have been bruised."

"However, coincidences do happen."

"The only alternative to its being an accident is that Mrs. Smith pushed him, but …"

Wing was interrupted by Watson, "No, she's far too frail to have pushed him down the alley. It would have had to have been one hell of a push as it would have to have been done from near the top of the alley." He checked his notes. "Neither the witness or the driver said they saw anyone at this end of the alley."

Wing nodded, "That worried me too, until I saw the hand cart in the barn."

"She might have earlier pushed him downstairs in an unsuccessful attempt to kill him, or she might just have hit him over the head to confuse him. Then she could have helped him onto the cart, propped him up on the handle, and then pushed it down the alley. The wall at the bottom would have stopped it running onto the road. No-one would have seen something as small as that cart, as all eyes would have been on Mr. Smith."

"But, if I were planning a murder, I'd have to make sure that *everything* went to plan. I'd practise the timing until I had it just right, and then do the real thing. No, what worried me was how she could have arranged for him to arrive in front of the lorry with such perfect timing … especially bearing in mind that she couldn't have actually heard the lorry."

Watson nodded, and pointed to his ears, making the same strange signs that Mr. Standish had, "No, of course, she couldn't have heard a lorry coming."

Wing continued, "I remember reading about Beethoven. He was profoundly deaf when he wrote some of his greatest music. He used to sense the music by interpreting reverberations through wood and other objects." Wing wasn't sure he'd got it quite right, but it was something like that.

"Could Mrs. Smith have done that, too? I mean, a lorry is much heavier than a piano."

"But something had been worrying me for a while. Then I remembered that mirror on the wall amongst the ivy, and I realised that it was that. If the alley hasn't been used for anything other than pedestrians for some time (and that low wall at the end is pretty old), then why is there a mirror that's obviously almost brand-new up there on the wall? Pedestrians would hardly have any need of it, as they could check if there were traffic coming by looking around the edge of the house. It looks more like some kitchen or vanity mirror that one might buy from a pound shop, certainly not durable enough to be used outside the house."

"And that might explain why Felicity said Mrs. Smith seemed most upset when she said she could make the telephone call from the cab. Felicity didn't need to leave 'the scene of the crime,' so Mrs. Smith wasn't able to remove the mirror secretly there and then."

As if on cue, Mrs. Smith poked her head out from the alley. She seemed satisfied that there was nobody about.

She moved the dustbin, clambered up onto it quite lithely for her age, and removed the mirror. Back on the ground, she seemed unsure what to do with it. Then she opened the dustbin, dropped it in, and put the dustbin lid back into place.

Detective Wing switched off the video recorder in his car.

"Got her!"

"I think we had better have another chat, er, face-to-face, with Mrs. Smith. What her motive is we'll have to ask, but I don't think getting a bypass was the main reason."

"It wouldn't surprise me if that were in her mind as a bonus, though!"

Interval

Having fulfilled her contractual obligations, Heather Davies collected her bag and rushed out of the room as fast as she could. As she passed though the door, Adrian Holland was just coming back from the toilet.

He noticed everyone looking in his direction, and quickly checked that his zip was up.

Reassured, he tried to continue to his seat, but found his sleeve being tugged by a smiling Professor Guiteras.

"It's your turn, Ade," he ordered.

Another Brick in the Wall

Steignquay, like most small seaside holiday resorts in Britain these days, was struggling to stay in business.

In an attempt to stop the more-than-gradual defection of its traditional holiday-makers to more Mediterranean climes, for publicity purposes it had arranged a twinning with one of the less-prestigious resorts not too far from the French Riviera. Many members of the Council had travelled there to "strengthen the ties," although very few (one actually) had made the reciprocal journey. The sign one encountered on arriving at the small coastal town had had "Twinned with," together with the name of the French resort misspelled, appended to it, in fact in larger letters than "Steignquay" itself. The old legend "Welcomes Careful Drivers" had been totally obscured by it, largely on the premise that, as long as they spent money whilst they were in town, nobody really worried about the visitors' driving abilities.

One young councillor had taken the bold step of renaming the Promenade "Le Cornichon." Only one councillor had actually bothered to look it up, and had complained that, rather than allude to some dramatic cliff highway in the South of France, it is in fact French for a gherkin. The original instigator had not batted an eyelid, but had replied that of course he knew this, and it was intended as a subtle play on words for those who understood these things, as the Promenade was indeed slightly curved, mostly green, and stank of vinegar for most of the year.

At the height of the season, the promenade, which stretched for over a mile between the two piers, was alive with day-trippers. Bright colours were everywhere, and the air was filled with the sounds of people being happy, both from the tourists and the local vendors. Donkeys brayed on the beach, children threw up below the West Pier, the litter bins overflowed with discarded half-filled trays of off-colour shrimps, and the "Vacancies Still Available" signs gathered dust in guest-house attics.

August had been glorious that year.

It was now the end of November.

Had the donkeys still been on the beach, their braying would have been drowned by the sounds of the huge breakers smashing against the already-beleaguered pier supports. The litter bins still overflowed with the discarded shrimp trays, but purely because they would not be emptied until the grand clear-up at the start of the next season (Works Department Manager Major 'Tanganyika' Wellington-Davies was personally in charge of 'Operation Clean Sweep' on the first day of every August). The "Vacancies Still Available" signs still gathered dust in guest-house attics, as no-one thought there was any point in hanging them up.

The litter that had been mercilessly blown around the promenade all last month had now been firmly pinned down by the persistent rain. Parasols, wind-breaks, and various other items of beach impedimenta still lay scattered around St. Tropez Gardens.

Some of the sea-front buildings had even been boarded up for the winter, including Steignquay's famous aquarium ("Visit Oceanland, and Learn Respect for the Sea - also Visit our Seafood Restaurant").

In fact, the whole of the sea-front presented a damp and dismal aspect, especially during the evening. It was now ten fifteen, and there was hardly a light to be seen along the famous Arcade Mile. Even the street-lamps were only half-heartedly doing their job.

In the little streets and lanes that ran behind the promenade, away from the full force of the wind and the sea, things were a little more lively, but only slightly so.

Smuggler's Lane was a small ancient crescent that ran around the back of the aptly-named Winter Gardens. The Lane had been called Victoria Lane (and nicknamed Turd Lane by the local children) until renamed by the Council in 1978 in an effort to make it more romantic and socially-desirable. It was still called Turd Lane by the local children.

Halfway along the lane, another, smaller, unnamed lane led off away from the sea-front. At the corner was a small and rather dingy public-house, 'The Smuggler's Arms.' This had been renamed at the same time as the Lane, and was originally called 'The Bloated Barrister,' apparently because of a particularly expensive piece of litigation in which a former landlord had been involved. The pub had no discernible connection with smuggling whatsoever, and, indeed, it seemed unlikely that there was ever very much in the way of marine activity at all in the region, owing to the large number of rocks in the bay. In any case, there had never been any real need for smuggling, as the area was well-provided for by a considerable number of substantial breweries, which had in the past had little in the way of taxes levied on their products owing to the rather corrupt local law enforcement (which had then been praised by the Government for its success in keeping down the level of alcohol smuggled into the area).

The unnamed lane was rather steep and the rain coursed down here at breakneck speed. Opposite 'The Smuggler's Arms' was a derelict shop, boarded up semi-permanently. Its guttering was clearly clogged up with vegetation, because rain flowed freely down its walls, soaking the figure of an old man, impeccably dressed in rather an antiquated style. He was leaning up against the brickwork, his eyes closed, but gradually he slid down the wall to lie in the gutter. The rain flowed over him, and then, now mingled with some of his blood, continued its way down towards the promenade and the sea.

D.I. Cramp stood in the rain outside 'The Smuggler's Arms.' He looked up at the sign creaking in the seemingly perpetual wind. The artist had painted the face so that it appeared even more evil than those in the other local pub-signs for 'The Green Man,' 'The Excise Man,' and even 'The Devil Incarnate,' this last-named having been once owned by a religious man who hated the demon drink but liked the profit margin and who wanted to try and escape accusations of hypocrisy. It was painfully clear that the sign had only been slightly altered to accommodate the change of name of the pub, and that the evil visage was in fact that of the barrister.

"I don't think we need to wait for the autopsy on this one," he sighed to his assistant, Herbert Burberry. The brick by the side of the body was all too clearly the weapon that had caused the bloody, but clean, wound on Major Robin Proctor's head.

Burberry nodded. "I've interviewed his friends in the pub. All four are in the clear, as the Major left the pub around 10.15, as he did every Thursday, and his friends all sat together until a John Wilson got up to leave and saw the Major's body from the doorway. He was already dead when three of them reached the body. The fourth stayed in the pub and phoned for an ambulance."

"So, where did our murderer get the brick from?" asked Cramp, looking around.

"I've already checked that. It matches those in a little pile of two bricks stacked up against the wall there." Burberry indicated some bricks under a small high window set into the wall of the pub. Here the wall was partly sheltered from the rain by some overhanging eaves.

"Don't you think it's more likely that the murderer originally took them from that large pile of identical bricks over there?" Cramp said, pointing to what looked like the remains of on old outhouse behind the pub.

Burberry nodded, a little sullenly.

"So, can we make any educated guesses about what happened here?" asked Cramp.

"Er, maybe" replied Burberry, playing for time.

"Let's see. If the murderer had been lying in wait for the Major, who it appears always left the pub at around the same time, he might have waited in the dry under the eaves there. And he might have retrieved the bricks from the back of the pub with the intention of standing on them to peer through that window into the bar. It should give a clear view of the table where the Major was sitting. That way he would have known when the Major was leaving."

Burberry nodded quietly.

"Anything else?" asked Cramp.

Burberry looked sheepish, and stayed silent.

"Don't you think we might be able to make a rough assessment of the murderer's minimum height by assuming that the window would be at least at the same level as his eyes when he was standing on the bricks?"

Burberry thought and then nodded, gradually increasing the amplitude of each nod until even he realised he looked rather silly. He made a final definite nod, and then went off to take the required measurements. Cramp felt he should be able to trust him to do that at least.

"Right," Burberry said, returning with a soggy tape measure and more confidence, "I've taken the measurements. The bricks, which are quite old, are each three inches high, but I can stand on the two bricks and just see the table at which the Major and his cronies were sitting. So our murderer must be at least my height, and I'm six foot. I mean, he hardly would have stood on tiptoe whilst balancing on the bricks, especially with such a large choice just around the corner."

Cramp nodded, "Okay. Well, I think we can discount an aimless random killing. I'm convinced our killer lay in wait for the Major specifically. And it's no mugging ..." Cramp held the Major's untouched wallet aloft. "Let's leave everyone to tidy up here. If you've got the names and addresses of those in the pub - everyone that is, not just the Major's friends - let's go home. We've an early start tomorrow at ..." he consulted an address in the wallet, "... The Bide-a-Wee Retirement Home."

Cramp thought it sounded like a correction centre for sufferers from enuresis.

Next morning, as Burberry was driving him to the Bide-a-Wee Retirement Home, Cramp sat musing, not just about the murder itself, but about the unusually busy winter they were having.

Normally, there were no crimes of any significance outside the busy summer month, but there were currently three crimes he had to investigate. Apart from the early demise of the Major, there was also a flasher with a penchant for exposing himself to young children in the most terrifying and threatening way, and a burglary at a semi-stately home nearby.

If this were a novel, all three crimes would ultimately be discovered to be linked, perhaps perpetrated by the same person, but this was real life.

These other two crimes would now have to take a back seat until the murderer had been apprehended.

Bide-a-Wee was a bleak modern red-brick building with few windows. It looked more like a prison for fairly trustworthy inmates.

Cramp and Burberry were met by Mrs. Dewhurst, a large domineering woman with immense bosoms (the singular word hardly seemed appropriate). Cramp thought that she looked as if she had been provided for a film by a very unimaginative casting department.

"The Major's room?" she boomed, "That's over here." She guided them to a room at the end of the main corridor off the reception area. "We had to move him here, together with his unit, as he called his group of friends. They tended to make a lot of noise, I'm afraid. It upset the other inmates." She laughed loudly and unnaturally. "That's a little joke we have here."

Her rapid change into an obviously-false bonhomie was sudden, unexpected, and not very tasteful. It was a few seconds before Cramp had recovered sufficiently to ask a question.

"Was the Major close to anyone here apart from his, er, unit? Do you know if he had any enemies?" This last comment was meant to have been said in a throwaway style, but would have fooled nobody.

Mrs. Dewhurst took a deep intake of breath and drew herself up to her full height (which would probably have been about the same had she been lying on her back). "I can assure you he didn't have any enemies here." Cramp noted that the word "here" was heavily stressed, implying that she felt sure he must have had plenty of enemies somewhere else outside her jurisdiction. "He was only really close to his three friends, whom he seemed to regard as a small and irregular military unit of which he was in complete charge. His batman, as he liked to call him, was Dobbins, who was utterly devoted to him, although I think it was someone else for whom he'd batmanned ..." she frowned slightly at the rather dubious verb "... During the War. He has this room, next to the Major's."

"In the two rooms across the way are William Bumford and Madge Burns. I have to say I was always surprised the way William fitted in so well with the Major, as they were from totally different backgrounds and social strata. Madge would have been more on the Major's social level. She's a very well-preserved lady in her early sixties, certainly the youngest at Bide-a-Wee, but, well, her mind isn't in the same condition as the rest of her, shall we say. Would you like to interview them?"

Cramp nodded unenthusiastically.

The three had clearly been told to wait in their rooms until interviewed by the police. The interviews should have been fairly short, but they became rather rambling owing to the ages of those involved, and the two policemen didn't leave the building until lunchtime.

All three had said they had been in the building the whole of the previous evening. Apparently, they rarely went out unless the Major had organised something for them, and, anyway, they had to be in by nine unless they had made a previous arrangement with Mrs. Dewhurst, otherwise all the outer doors were well secured.

They had all confirmed that none of them had any reason to wish ill upon the Major.

"What do you think?" Cramp enquired of Burberry as they left the Home. Then, without waiting for an answer, he added, "I wouldn't put anything past that Mrs. Dewhurst, but there only seems to be the Major's three friends who had any involvement with him, and they seem harmless enough. Dobbins, his batman, seemed positively devoted to him. His military training seems to be standing him in good stead, but I felt he must have had a good cry in private at some time. Do you think there's a possibility of a ménage à trois ... or even quatre?"

Burberry looked more blank than usual.

"Anyway," Cramp continued, "No-one in the Home could have gone out and returned after nine without Mrs. Dewhurst knowing, so we'll have to look elsewhere."

Burberry made a half-hearted, non-committal grunt. He had been noting things down in his notebook. Not one of the three of them was anywhere near six feet in height. In fact, Dobbins was five nine, William was about five feet six inches, and the fair Madge a mere five two. Mrs. Dewhurst was even shorter than Madge. He shook his head sadly.

"With a bit of luck," Cramp said, cheering up a little, "Our Major was the flasher and we've only got two crimes left to solve."

Steignquay Diamond Jubilee Park was basking itself in one of the rare winter days of semi-dryness. It had been named, not to celebrate the successfully-long reign of some recent monarch, but to commemorate the wedding anniversary of some long-forgotten councillor.

There were few people in the park, but all those there seemed to be enjoying themselves, with the exception of young James Burke, who was crying his eyes out and complaining that he wanted to go to the toilet. He was at that awkward age where he was too old for his mother to take him into the ladies' section of the public toilets, and yet too young to go to the gents' himself. His mother, Juanita, duly took his hand and led him to the rear of a large sycamore tree, where, as usual, everything took considerably longer than one would have expected.

It was whilst she was behind the tree that she became aware of a commotion amongst her remaining three children. Remembering warnings about an elderly man exposing himself to young children, she left James to his own devices and wandered around the bushes to see what was going on. Juanita was the sort to imagine anything terrible that she heard on the news happening to her own children. And this case seemed a particularly unpleasant one. The flasher uttered obscene phrases, seemed particularly proud of what he was doing and of what he had, and seemed highly aggressive. She had meticulously memorised what little description they had of him and his clothing.

To her horror, her worst fears were confirmed.

A fairly elderly gentleman, wearing clothes which exactly fitted those in the description given by the Police, was standing with his back to her. Clearly oblivious to her presence, he was holding his coat open and facing the children, who, it has to be said, looked rather intrigued, instead of shocked and horrified. Juanita shouted loudly.

The gentleman spun around. To Juanita's surprise, although he had his coat open in the traditional flasher's stance, he did not seem to be exposing much. His zip was done up, and there seemed nothing really untoward going on at all.

Nevertheless, he yelled out in horror, and turned and hobbled off towards the park gates. Juanita noticed that he ran rather unsteadily.

She thought of chasing him and was quite sure she could have caught him, but instead she ran straight over to her children to comfort them. They seemed not to require any great degree of comforting, and Brigitte giggled and said "I was waiting for him, Mum." She opened her hand to show a small pair of scissors she must have stolen from a drawer at home.

Just then, a shrill voice called out from behind the tree, "I've wet my pants, Mum."

D.I. Cramp sighed, "So we've still got three criminals to find, eh, Burberry?"

Burberry nodded, "You were really hoping the Major was our flasher, weren't you?"

"Not really. It would just have made life so much easier for us."

"The Major's not the sort, I'm sure: 'The Honour of the Regiment' and all that.

"So what have we got?" Cramp asked rhetorically, before continuing almost immediately.

"Four friends in the pub, none of whom had a motive and none of whom could have left the pub and hit the Major over the head."

Burberry interrupted, for once constructively. "I've interviewed the one close relative the Major has in this area. Almost all his family seem to have emigrated en bloc to New Zealand in the sixties." He flipped open his notepad quite dramatically, but didn't seem to bother to refer to it at any point. "Percy Proctor lives about ten miles away to the east in Slimehaven. He's none too fit, and doesn't go anywhere these days unless he has his helper with him. Neither he nor his helper would seem to have had a motive, as there's no money involved in the Major's demise. Percy doesn't have an alibi, but his helper seems to have a fairly good one. Percy had a wife, now deceased, and two children, twins, living in Scotland, but they can be discounted in terms of alibis and distance."

Cramp nodded. "So that leaves us with the three friends in the Home, who may have had a motive - jealousy, love for the same woman, something like that - but no opportunity, as they couldn't have got past Mrs. Dewhurst's curfew ...."

"And there's nobody else we've found who even knew of the Major's existence. But it can't have been a mugging or a random killing."

Cramp made a strange clicking noise with his tongue, as he usually did when he was thinking deeply. He picked up the phone and dialled the Bide-a-Wee Retirement Home and asked for Mrs. Dewhurst.

"Have any of your folk asked for a curfew pass during the last month?"

Although some distance from the phone, Burberry could hear the reply quite distinctly. Having been forced to apologise for his use of the term 'curfew pass,' Cramp learned that there had only been one such request, from a Mrs. Cosgrove who wished to go to the local theatre for a sing-along screening of 'The Sound of Music.' Mrs. Dewhurst hadn't been too sure because of all the Nazis in it, but had reluctantly sanctioned the visit.

Cramp put back the phone, and turned to Burberry. "All right, but if the Major went out every Thursday and returned around ten-thirty without Mrs. Dewhurst's permission, he at least had a way around the curfew rules. Being a military man, he probably would have thought of it as a challenge. And, if he knew, I'm sure his three fellow inmates would have."

"That's all very well, but the three of them are all the wrong height," objected Burberry.

Cramp clicked ruminatively for a few seconds, then began to look a little happier.

"You seem to be our expert on heights, Burberry. How tall was the Major?"

Burberry was clearly proud to be able to provide that information, "Exactly six foot, the same as I am. Oh God! You don't think he was the one who piled those bricks up to look through the window of the pub, do you? He seems to be the only one of the right height in the whole business."

"I hardly think that the Major would have clambered up on those bricks to look in through the pub window to watch himself, Burberry."

"However, I do have a solution which I think explains everything."

He smiled uncharacteristically.

D.I. Cramp closed his eyes and leaned back in his rocking swivel chair with the leatherette foot-rest. He had told everyone it had been provided for him by his grateful employers, but he had actually bought it in a sale in 'Chairs Is We' last January. He had now more or less mastered its use, and had not fallen backwards off it since the week before last.

"The thing that seemed to me most unusual about all the recent events around here was how different the flasher seemed to be this time."

"Although his physical description was virtually identical in terms of general appearance and clothing, his whole demeanour was so different. In fact, the whole affair seems to have been so, well, half-hearted."

"Things seemed to have gone off at half-cock," interrupted Burberry, even less constructively than usual.

Cramp ignored him, indeed probably hadn't even heard him. "The first few times our flasher struck, he seemed one of the nastiest exponents of a particularly nasty crime. This last time he looked the part, but seemed too timid and almost disinterested. Anyway, he didn't really commit any crime at all. The kids seemed to think of him more as a children's entertainer, Uncle Willy or whatever, and thoroughly enjoyed the show. That may be because children today are like that, but, the first few times the flasher struck, the kids would have been no different, and they were absolutely terrified."

"It really did seem as if he were someone else acting out a role. And it was no copycat crime: his heart just didn't seem to be in it. It was almost as if he were standing in for someone ill or on holiday, as if he were doing it out of a sense of duty."

"And why did he run off so awkwardly? Juanita Burke said he seemed unsteady on his feet, and that she thought she could easily have caught him. That could fit in with the idea of the real villain being unavailable, and someone else having to wear his shoes and clothes. If the stand-in had had different-sized feet, then he probably would have run awkwardly."

"But why would anyone, especially someone who clearly had no heart for that sort of thing, copy or borrow the real flasher's clothes and imitate such a distasteful crime?"

"The most likely thing I can think of is that the original criminal had had his career cut short, and a friend perhaps had decided to perpetrate one more crime in order to divert suspicion away from him."

"And who can you think of who has been incapacitated recently, and who had a loyal follower?"

Burberry beamed, "I'm way ahead of you, Sir. If the Major were the flasher and his batman got to hear of it and tried to force him to stop without success, I wouldn't put it past him to kill the Major for the sake of the good name of the Regiment, and then stage one more performance so that no suspicion could fall on the Major."

Cramp nodded. "I'm sure Juanita Burke would recognise him in a line-up. I mean, there wasn't much else for her to look at, was there?"

"Anyway, maybe we'd only have to challenge Dobbins with it, and he'd confess."

"But I think you've forgotten one small thing, Sir." Burberry's expression could best be described as triumphant.

"We know almost the exact height of our murderer from the bricks piled up outside the pub. It's six foot, give or take a few fractions of an inch. Unfortunately only the Major seems to have been anywhere near that height. Dobbins is three inches shorter."

Cramp looked a little contemptuously at Burberry.

"And what about the brick that killed the Major? Where do you think Dobbins got that from?"

Epilogue

Professor Guiteras watched out of his study window as the last of the students retreated around the corner of the street.

It had been a fairly good year, he reflected. The students' stories were better than at his previous party, which had represented the nadir in quality as far as he was concerned, and had almost deterred him from holding further soirées. He had only organised the party this year because of a shortfall in his finances and a general lack of creativity on his part.

Now, all the students had gone, and his wife had retired to bed some hours ago. He had told her he would do the washing up, but, in fact, he merely wanted her out of the way, and had no intention of venturing near the kitchen.

His creative juices were flowing at long last.

He sat down at his computer desk. The computer had long ago been consigned to the back room: the spell-check facility continually plagued him by underlining all his Spanish words in red, and he couldn't find out how to disable it. His old typewriter now resided on the computer desk.

Yes, it wasn't a bad crop of stories this year, he mused.

He inserted a sheet of paper into the typewriter, and started typing in Spanish.

"The Return of Inspector Pirat"

"One"

"When Inspector Pirat got to the top of the main chair-lift from Liria Village to the summit of Mount Merida, he found a large group of people gathered around the top of another chair-lift to his right."

"Knowing it would be wiser to ignore the situation completely and to continue to the main skiing pistes to his left, he nevertheless sauntered off towards the crowd, perhaps through idle curiosity, perhaps because of the professional interest of a police officer on holiday. "Plain ruddy nosy" would have been the phrase, suitably bowdlerised, his staff would have used.

"The chair-lift was stopped, and a rather plump lady in a striking pink-and-white ski outfit was lying on the ground underneath one of the chairs. Someone with at least some medical experience (perhaps another meddlesome professional on holiday, Inspector Pirat thought to himself) was crouched over the body, examining it in a rather brisk, perfunctory manner. It seemed dead ..."